# Home Is the Place

# Home Is the Place

## The Fourth Generation

### ANN M. MARTIN

SCHOLASTIC INC.

ISBN 978-0-545-83190-1

10 9 8 7 6 5 4 3 2 1    15 16 17 18 19

Printed in the U.S.A.    23
This edition first printing, January 2015

The text type was set in Baskerville MT.
Book design by Elizabeth B. Parisi

This book is for Lily, EJ,
and the next generation

# Chapter 1

"Happy birthday, Georgie Girl!"

Georgia Noble rolled over in bed and smiled at her mother, who had cracked open the door to her room and poked her head inside.

"Don't tell me you weren't already awake," said her mother. She opened the door wider. "Last night you were so excited you couldn't fall asleep."

"I was awake," Georgia admitted, then yawned. "A little bit, anyway." She stretched her arms above her head and tried to decide if being six felt any different than being five. She wasn't sure yet.

Her mother sat on the end of the bed and tweaked Georgia's toes through the covers.

Georgia stuffed her pillow behind her back and sat up. She glanced at the window that faced onto Vandeventer Avenue in downtown Princeton, and next to it at the coat-rack shaped like a giant crayon, from which hung a fraying bunny suit and her collection of princess dresses. She wondered if these were five-year-old things (baby things) or whether they were okay for six-year-olds, too.

"Mommy?"

"Yes?"

"When you were little this was your room, too, wasn't it?"

"Yes, it was."

"Did you still play dress-up when you were six?"

"Absolutely," her mother replied.

Georgia considered this. "I like waking up in your room."

Georgia's mother smiled. "Remember last summer when we visited the beach house in Maine and you slept in the upstairs room? That was Great-Grandma Abby's room when she was a girl. Nana Dana has woken up in that room, and I have, and so have you. Four generations of women in our family, all waking up in the same room, looking at the same view out the window."

Georgia found this confusing so she changed the subject. "What color did you frost the cupcakes for my school party?" she asked. "The boys won't want pink, you know. Even if today is Valentine's Day. Red frosting would be okay, but not pink."

Her mother laughed. "Half are pink and half are red, so I think you're safe. Now — look out the window if you want a surprise."

Georgia sat up, raised the shade, and peered outside. "It's snowing!" she exclaimed. "Oh no! Mommy, this isn't a good surprise. What if school is closed? What about my party?"

"School's open. Don't worry. This is just a little snow."

It was actually a little snow on top of a lot of snow. The winter had been very stormy, and the schools in Princeton, New Jersey, had closed six times so far.

"Are you sure?" asked Georgia nervously. She watched a snowplow grind along in front of her house.

"Positive. Now get up and get dressed. It's Valentine's Day and your birthday."

"The same as for my great-great-aunt Adele?"

Georgia had never met Adele, who had died long before Georgia had been born, but she had heard many, many stories about her.

"The same as for your great-great-aunt Adele. Now get dressed."

Georgia waited until her mother had left the room before she got out of bed. Then she checked her door to make sure it was closed tightly, to keep out her brother Richard, who was seven. Satisfied, she stood before her closet and chose a pair of jeans, a red shirt, and a red sweater. She put them on quickly, shivering in the chilly room, then peered into her mirror and considered her hair, which was dark blond and very thick. "Hard to manage," her mother often said. "You can barely get a comb through it." So Georgia didn't bother with the comb. She simply pulled her hair out of her face and tied a red ribbon around it.

She was ready to be six years old.

The Nobles gathered for breakfast in the kitchen of their big Victorian house. Georgia, Richard, and their parents sat at the table, and Henry, who was just two, was seated in his high chair, legs kicking the air vigorously while he sang a made-up song about a snowplow.

Georgia's father kissed her on the top of her head and placed a small wrapped box next to her plate. "Happy birthday, Georgie Girl," he said.

Before Georgia knew it, her family was singing the birthday song. Her mother sang softly, unsure of her own voice. Her father sang loudly and off-key, not caring. Henry sang, "Happy birthday, dear snowplow." And above them all, Georgia could hear Richard's voice: "Happy birthday to you, you live in a zoo. You look like a monkey and smell like one, too!"

"You know, that's rude to monkeys," Georgia said to her brother when the song was over. "Besides, maybe monkeys like the way they smell. Maybe when they make fun of each other they say, 'You smell like a boy!'"

Richard jumped up from the table. "I do not smell!"

"Ahem," said Mr. Noble, and Richard sat down again.

"Mommy, can we walk to school in the snow?" asked Georgia, thinking of her new green rubber boots, the ones that weren't warm, but that looked like frogs, complete with hooded eyes and wide mouths.

Her mother shook her head. "Not with two boxes of cupcakes for your party. We have to drive."

Georgia glanced sideways at Mrs. Noble. "If we didn't have to carry the cupcakes could we walk in the snow?"

"I don't know, honey."

"You never let us walk!" exclaimed Georgia.

"Yes, she does. We always walk," said Richard.

"Not alone."

"You're too young to walk without an adult," said her mother in the clipped way that Georgia knew meant she didn't want to have this discussion.

But Georgia couldn't help herself. "Leslie walks without an adult," she replied. Leslie Jordan, Georgia's next-door neighbor, was her Vandeventer Avenue best friend, although not her school best friend.

"Leslie walks with her big brother. And before you say another word, let me remind you that Leslie's big brother is eleven, not seven."

"But —"

"Why don't you open the present?" interrupted her father. "This is just a little something for now. You can open the rest of your presents tonight."

It was to be a two-party birthday — the Valentine birthday party at school and a family party that night when all the grandparents arrived. Georgia sighed. She liked presents, of course. But what she really wanted was a bit more independence. From her mother anyway. It seemed that Mrs. Noble, who wrote books for grown-ups in her home office, was always hovering somewhere nearby, following Georgia the short distance across the yard to Leslie's house, watching her and her brothers through the kitchen window as they played in the backyard, even checking on them in the middle of the night. And she was always setting limits and making restrictions. Richard didn't seem to mind the restrictions so much — often he just went ahead and did whatever he wanted, paying for it later — and Henry was too little to care. But Georgia felt like a teensy, little person trapped in a snow-globe world, and she wanted out.

Feeling almost reluctant, Georgia opened the box, which contained a silver necklace with a heart pendant. "Thank you," she said. She had asked for a silver necklace with G-E-O-R-G-I-A spelled out on it, but her mother had reminded her how dangerous it was to wear anything that told a stranger your name. "What if someone saw you on the street wearing that necklace," she had said, "and he called, 'Hi, Georgia! Your mom told me to pick you up from school.' What would you do?"

"I wouldn't go with him because he would be a stranger," Georgia had replied.

But her mother had shaken her head and Georgia had known that the name necklace would have to wait until she was older and could earn enough money to buy it herself.

The drive to school — the very same school that Georgia's mother, Francie, had attended when she was a girl — was slow and slippery, and Georgia watched a car glide gracefully off the street ahead of them and into a snow bank, where it remained stuck, tires spinning noisily. Georgia's mother set her mouth in a firm line and drove on wordlessly. "I'm glad that's over," she said when they finally reached the school parking lot.

Mrs. Noble lifted Henry out of the car, and Georgia and Richard each reached for a platter of cupcakes. They walked into school, their boots dripping slush behind them, Georgia smelling wet wool and damp jackets as they made their way to her kindergarten room.

"I'm here!" she announced to Mrs. Frederickson.

"Wonderful," replied her teacher, laughing. "Why don't you put the cupcakes on the table in the back?"

Richard set down his platter in a great big hurry and ran for his first-grade classroom. "See you, baby!" he called to Georgia as he fled.

She ignored him. "Mommy, you'll come back in time for the party, won't you? You'll be done writing by then?"

"Absolutely. Henry and I will be back at two."

Georgia looked fondly at the pink and red cupcakes. She looked out the windows at the snow falling lightly on the playground. She forgot about the G-E-O-R-G-I-A necklace and limits and restrictions and began to feel excited. Two parties, and a visit from her grandparents, all five of them. It was good to be six.

At her school party, Georgia ate a pink cupcake and showed Henry off to her classmates. He sang the snowplow song and demonstrated how he could stick out his tongue and touch his nose with it. Having him there was almost as good as having a dog. The only thing that could have made the party better would have been Georgia's father, but he taught fourth grade at Littlebrook, the elementary school across town, and couldn't leave his students.

By the time Georgia and Richard and Henry were riding home with their mother, the sun had come out and the new snow was melting in the street.

"Can I build a snowman?" Georgia asked as her mother parked the car in the garage.

"If you stay in the backyard with Richard," Mrs. Noble replied.

"But I want to build it in the frontyard so everyone can see it."

"And I don't want to build a snowman at all," added Richard.

"Then can I go to Leslie's?" asked Georgia.

"Sure. Call her to make sure it's okay. I'll walk you over."

Georgia let out an enormously loud sigh. "Can't you just watch me from the front steps?"

Mrs. Noble unfastened her seat belt and turned around to look at her daughter. "Georgia."

"Okay."

"Okay what?"

"Okay, I'm not going then."

Georgia pouted in her room. She slid the offensive heart necklace to the back of the top desk drawer. The desk, which Georgia was proud of, was white with vines and leaves and fairies painted on it. She knew that her grandfather had painted it for her mother when Francie had been Georgia's age. Georgia ran her hand across the top and tried to imagine Papa Matthew at work in the third-floor room that had been his studio, before he and Nana Dana had gotten divorced and sold the house.

At six o'clock Georgia heard a knock on her door. "Almost party time, Georgie Girl!" called her father.

Georgia felt her heart soar. It was amazing how quickly her mood could change. She ran downstairs and proceeded to open the door each time the bell rang — when her father's parents arrived from northern New Jersey, when Papa Matthew and his wife, Maura, arrived from their house near the Princeton University campus, and when Nana Dana arrived from New York City. Georgia gathered the presents they brought and set them on the table in the living room.

Each time she added another gift to the pile, Henry asked hopefully, "Is that for me?" And each time Georgia answered patiently, "No, it's for me, but we can share," and Henry seemed satisfied.

The menu for dinner had been chosen entirely by Georgia. Her mother had not changed a single thing. Spaghetti with meatballs, artichokes, and chocolate cake. Everyone, even Richard, agreed that it was the perfect menu. After dinner, Georgia longed to be allowed to flick the switch that would operate the garbage disposal, sending the artichoke leaves into a glorious, ground-up fury, but Mrs. Noble didn't like the children anywhere near the sink when the disposal was on.

Georgia decided not to spoil the evening by asking about something she knew was not allowed. Instead she opened her gifts. The only thing of interest to Henry was an intricate-looking toy called a Spirograph, which Nana Dana claimed Georgia's mother had loved when she was six years old. At nine o'clock, as everyone was yawning and the guests were standing and stretching, Georgia's sixth birthday came to an end. She carried her pile of presents upstairs to her room, put on the new nightgown from Papa Matthew and Maura, and wondered what the rest of the year would bring.

# Chapter 2

*Tuesday, September 11th, 2001*

Georgia, halfway through her breakfast, set down her cereal spoon and gazed through the open kitchen window at the backyard.

"What's the matter, Georgie Girl?" asked her mother. "Not hungry?"

Georgia smiled. "I'm hungry. I'm just thinking about today. It still feels like summer, even though school started. It's warm out, and we're eating cantaloupe." She glanced under the table at her feet. "*And* I'm wearing sandals." She spooned Cheerios into her mouth and said, "Today is my fifth day of first grade."

"And yesterday was your fourth. Are you going to say that *every* day?" asked Richard from across the table.

"Am I going to say that every day is my fifth day of first grade?"

Richard scowled at her. "*No.* Are you going to announce —"

"Kids," said their father. "Please."

Georgia fell silent. She didn't care what her brother said. It was a beautiful day out, and she and Leslie Jordan had plans to write a play about princesses after school. Georgia was going to put on her Snow White costume and Leslie was going to put on her Ariel costume, and they were going to sit under the elm tree in Georgia's backyard and write a play to perform for their families. They might charge admission.

Georgia and Leslie had been in different kindergarten classrooms, but this year they were both in Mr. Brice's first-grade class, so now Leslie was Georgia's school best friend in addition to her Vandeventer Avenue best friend. Every day they walked to school with Richard and either Mrs. Jordan or Georgia's mother and Henry. (Leslie's big brother went to the middle school now. Georgia, Leslie, and Richard had all lobbied to walk to and from school without an adult, but the idea had been turned down by both of Georgia's parents *and* the Jordans, so at least Georgia's mom wasn't the only unreasonable parent on the street.)

"What a lovely blue sky," said Mrs. Noble that morning as she pushed Henry's stroller along the sidewalk.

Georgia, who was walking ahead with Leslie and Richard, proudly clutched her first-grade reader to her chest. She tipped her head back and said, "Not a single cloud. Not one. See? It still feels like summer. Like summer vacation."

Mrs. Noble stopped at the front door of the elementary school and let Georgia, Leslie, and Richard run inside to their classrooms on their own. "See you this afternoon!" she called.

Georgia and Leslie ran to Mr. Brice's room and found that he had opened all the windows. Written on the chalkboard in large cheery letters were the words:

HAPPY TUESDAY!

DAY #5 OF FIRST GRADE

"The perfect day for a nature walk," Mr. Brice said after the morning business had been attended to. "We'll go before lunch. But first, time for reading and math."

Georgia, who liked reading, read a story about a dog and a cat who were best friends, and then wrote a story about her own best friend, Leslie. Math began and Georgia was working her way down a page of addition problems, when a brief knock sounded on the door to the classroom and Mrs. Cierniak, another first-grade teacher, stuck her head inside and signaled to Mr. Brice. He leaned out into the hallway, whispered to Mrs. Cierniak, then sat down at his desk a few seconds later with an expression on his face that Georgia couldn't quite figure out.

This was the moment when Georgia's perfect summer day began to slide sideways.

Next the principal stopped in to speak with Mr. Brice.

Mr. Brice left his class alone for several minutes, which he had not done at all on the previous four days of first grade. When he returned, he was slipping his cell phone into his pocket.

Other teachers stopped in. Two of them were crying.

Georgia craned her neck forward until she could see into the hallway. Then she leaned across the aisle and whispered to Leslie, "There are a lot of teachers out there. They're talking on their cell phones." She took another look. "I think I see Maddy's mother." She glanced over her shoulder at Madeleine Trego. "Maddy doesn't look sick."

"Class," said Mr. Brice, and Georgia thought his voice was shaking, but she wasn't sure. "Please continue with your work sheets."

He said this even as Mrs. Trego let herself into the room, walked to Maddy's desk, and said quietly, "We're going home now."

Georgia raised her hand. "Mr. Brice? Did something happen?"

Mr. Brice looked as though he didn't want to answer the question. He pulled a handkerchief from his pocket and wiped his forehead. "Well," he said, "there's been a . . . a tragedy in New York City. And in Washington, DC."

Georgia frowned. New York City was fifty miles away. Washington, DC, was even farther. "Are we still going to go on our walk?" she wanted to know.

The door to Mr. Brice's room stood open, and four more parents arrived: Antony's father, Autumn's mother, and both of Shelby's parents. They spoke quietly to their children and urgently to one another, and then they left in a hurry. Antony, Autumn, and Shelby didn't even have time to push their chairs under their desks.

"Why are our parents coming?" asked Georgia, without bothering to raise her hand. At that moment her own mother hurried into the room, Henry on her hip.

"Come on, girls," she said to Georgia and Leslie. "Let's get Richard. We're going home."

"Me, too?" asked Leslie.

"But why?" asked Georgia, whose stomach was beginning to feel strange.

"I'll explain on the way."

Georgia didn't understand her mother's explanation. At least, she didn't understand why it meant that the parents were showing up at school and why the nature walk had been canceled.

"Something is happening. It seems like some sort of attack," said Georgia's mom as she steered her Subaru onto Vandeventer. She turned the car so quickly that Georgia knocked her head against Leslie's shoulder. "Two planes were flown into buildings in New York, and another plane was flown into the Pentagon in Washington. A fourth plane was hijacked —"

"Who's attacking us?" asked Richard.

"What's the Pentagon?" asked Georgia.

"Which buildings in New York?" asked Leslie.

Mrs. Noble glanced into the rearview mirror and her eyes briefly met Leslie's. "I'm not sure," she replied, and Georgia knew her mother was lying about not knowing which buildings. Then Mrs. Noble added, "Leslie, you're going to stay with us today."

"But who's attacking us?" asked Richard again.

"It isn't clear," said Mrs. Noble. "No one knows much."

Georgia's stomach, which was already feeling queasy, tightened unpleasantly. "Are they going to attack Princeton? Is that why you're bringing us home?"

Mrs. Noble pulled into the driveway and parked the car.

"I think we're safe here," she said. "But just in case, we'll stay inside for a while."

"Why can't I go home?" asked Leslie, looking across the yard at her house.

"Your mom's busy today. She has a lot of calls to make."

"Where's my brother?"

"He went home with Nazim." Mrs. Noble reached for Leslie's hand. "Come on in. We'll fix something special for lunch later."

"You know, my dad works in New York," said Leslie as she followed Georgia's mother inside. "In one of the very, very tall buildings called the Twin Towers. I visited him there once. We went up as high as we could and we saw all the way to California."

"You did not!" exclaimed Richard. "You can't see California from New York."

"Maybe it was Connecticut," said Leslie. "Anyway, we were very high up, and that's where my dad works. He takes the train from Princeton Junction every day," she added.

Georgia's mom set Henry down on the floor of the family room. "Can you be in charge of your brother, please?" she said to Richard and Georgia, and she disappeared into the kitchen. Georgia heard her turn on the little TV and she followed her mother curiously.

"Mom?" whispered Georgia.

Her mother was flicking from station to station and all Georgia could see were people running and screaming, tall buildings with smoke pouring from the upper floors, and stunned newscasters talking about the attack on the United States.

Georgia's eyes widened. "That's the attack?" she asked.

Her mother left the TV on and picked up the phone. She punched in a number, waited for a moment, and then said, "Damn," very softly.

"What's wrong?" asked Georgia. "Mom, my stomach doesn't feel good."

"Lie down for a bit then," her mother replied vaguely, and walked her back into the family room. "I want to make sure Nana Dana's okay, but the call won't go through."

"Why not?" asked Richard.

"Too many people trying to make calls, I guess. Everyone wants to check on the people they know in New York."

"Do you think my dad's okay?" asked Leslie.

Georgia's mom punched in another number, listened, and said, "Damn," again. She clicked the phone off and two seconds later it rang. "*Hello?* . . . Oh, Mom, thank goodness it's you. Are you all right? . . . Okay. . . . Good. . . . I'm home with the kids. I just picked them up from school. . . . Leslie's with us." She paused. "I mean, she's sitting right here — just a sec." Mrs. Noble took the phone back into the kitchen.

"I'm going home," Leslie announced suddenly.

Richard looked alarmed. He glanced at the kitchen, and then back at Leslie. To Georgia's surprise, his face softened. He touched Leslie's arm. "You'd better not," he said. "Mom said to stay here. Come on. Let's go to my room. We can all play with my Legos."

"*All* of us?" asked Georgia. "Even Henry?"

Richard nodded. "Yup. Come on."

Playing calmly in Richard's room with his Legos was such a novelty that Georgia's stomach settled, and eventually she realized she was hungry. "Can we go downstairs for lunch?" she asked Richard, as if he were in charge of the day.

Richard looked serious. He tiptoed to the top of the stairs and listened. "Yes," he said after a moment.

Lunch was tomato sandwiches and watermelon slices eaten on the porch, which was indeed special, but as soon as it was over, Mrs. Noble reached for the phone again. "I spoke with your aunt Kaycee," she announced to Georgia and Richard. "They're all fine. But I still haven't heard from — Listen, why don't you go back upstairs?"

Georgia, who could hear the TV playing in the kitchen, even though no one was listening to it, said hastily, "Yes, let's go back to Richard's room."

But at that moment the front door opened and her father strode inside.

"Daddy!" cried Georgia, and flung herself at him.

"Hi, Georgie Girl."

The phone rang then and Mrs. Noble answered it. "I'm just going to run next door," she whispered to Georgia's father after she'd hung up.

There were tears in her eyes.

The rest of the day passed slowly. The phone kept ringing. Then there were long periods of time when Georgia's father couldn't make any calls. Toward dinnertime, Leslie began to cry. At last Mrs. Jordan arrived to take her home. Georgia's mother remained next door.

Mr. Noble turned to Georgia and Richard once Leslie was gone. "Kids?" he said, and instructed them to sit on the couch in the living room. He sat down between them and was silent for a moment. At last he said, "Leslie's father works in one of the buildings that was attacked." He took their hands in his.

"One of the buildings that caught on fire and fell down?" asked Georgia.

"Yes."

"Did all the people in those buildings die?" Richard wanted to know.

"No. But a lot of them did. And no one has heard from Mr. Jordan yet. We think he would have gotten through to Leslie's mom somehow if he were okay. So there's a good chance that —"

Before Georgia's father could finish his sentence, Richard said, "Maybe he's just in the hospital! Maybe he got hurt really badly and he can't talk."

"Maybe," said Mr. Noble. "There's always hope."

At bedtime that night, which was later than usual, Georgia waited for her father to tuck her in.

"How long is Mom going to stay next door?" she asked as he perched beside her.

"A while longer. Maybe she'll spend the night. Leslie's mother needs company."

"Is there school tomorrow?"

"There's school for anyone who feels like going."

"What about the cars in the parking lot?"

"The cars in the parking lot?"

"When Mr. Spagnoli came by tonight, I heard him say that there were unclammed cars in the parking lot at the train station."

Georgia's father sighed. "Un*claimed* cars. Yes. Quite a few people from Princeton commute to New York City for work, like Leslie's father. They leave their cars in the lot at the station. Some of them didn't come home today so their cars are still there."

"They didn't come home because they died in New York?"

"Probably."

"Is Leslie's father's car there?"

"Yes."

"Leslie must be very sad."

Mr. Noble nodded.

"Maybe we'll write our princess play tomorrow," said Georgia. "That will cheer her up."

But as she lay in her bed that night, she thought not about Snow White and Ariel but about burning, falling buildings, and the cars in the parking lot at the train station.

# Chapter 3

*Monday, December 31st, 2001*

# Francie Goldberg Noble

Francie Noble stood in the kitchen in the early morning quiet and stared at the calendar on the refrigerator. The world outside the windows was pitch dark, as dark as midnight. Five thirty a.m. and she was the only one awake, her husband and children sleeping soundly upstairs. She felt as if she were the only one awake on her street, in her town, in the entire world.

Francie touched her finger to the last square on the last page of the calendar. December 31st, 2001. The final day of a year she would sooner forget. She sighed, removed the calendar from the fridge, and stuck it in the recycling box in the corner. Then she looked at the 2002 calendar that Georgia had given her for Christmas. Page after page of kittens. She left the calendar lying on the table and tiptoed upstairs to her daughter's bedroom.

Georgia always slept on her back, and under at least one blanket, no matter what the temperature.

Francie gazed at her. This girl. Her daughter. Her *daughter.* This little girl living in the room that had been her own when she'd been Georgia's age.

Francie's eyes roamed to the window by Georgia's bed. In a flash, twenty-two years fell away, and Francie was nine again, a fourth grader in Mr. Apwell's class. A panicked, bewildered girl checking the street below for a black station wagon, checking obsessively, over and over. Is it there? Is it there now? How about *now?* Is it safe to go outside?

Francie backed out of Georgia's room, leaned against the hallway wall, and slid to the floor. She sat there, forehead resting on her knees. She had never forgotten the man in the station wagon and she had never told her parents what had happened. She hadn't forgotten Erin Mulligan either, the girl who had been taken by the man in the station wagon just days after he had tried to lure Francie into his car. Erin, the girl Francie could have become, the girl who had captured Princeton's attention and then, when the search for her finally ended, had faded away.

How was a mother supposed to keep her children safe?

Francie tiptoed back downstairs and looked across the side yard at the Jordans' house. A light was on in their living room. So Francie wasn't the only one awake after all. Right next door, someone was already up. Probably Emilie, who was packing up the house, preparing to move, even though everyone had told her not to make any rash decisions until a year after her husband's death. But she couldn't stand to live in the house on Vandeventer without him. She had said so on the night of September 11th.

Francie returned to the kitchen and fastened Georgia's kitten calendar to the refrigerator.

"Mom, when will *we* be old enough to go to a New Year's Eve party?" Georgia asked that evening. Then she added, "You look pretty."

"Thank you," said Francie, who turned around to examine herself in the bathroom mirror. "Do you think these earrings are too big?"

"No, they're just right. But when can we go to a party?"

"You're going to have a party tonight. With Betsy."

Betsy was the seventeen-year-old babysitter who had a pierced nose. Even Richard liked her.

And Francie trusted her. Mostly. She had set up a Nanny Cam the first four times Betsy had babysat for Richard, Francie, and Henry. She had scrutinized the footage to make sure Betsy was following all of Francie's safety procedures, and that she wasn't secretly allowing strange men in the house.

"Honestly, honey, Betsy's references are great," George had said when Francie had first suggested the Nanny Cam to her husband. "She's sat for the Jordans and the Mayhews. Everybody loves her."

"You can't be too careful," Francie had replied.

Now Georgia began to jump up and down. "Really? We really get to have a party?"

"Absolutely," said Francie.

"Can we stay up until midnight?"

"You and Richard may, if you can stay awake."

"Yes!" cried Georgia, before hugging her mother around the waist.

The party at the McCloskeys' house was just the sort that Francie enjoyed. Some people were dressed up and some weren't. Some were standing in tight perfumy groups holding fancy cocktails, and some were sitting on the floor in front of the fireplace. Dinner was buffet style. A few people ate seated at the dining room table, but most ate in the living room, balancing plates on their laps.

Francie and her husband sat next to each other on a white couch, trying not to spill.

"Either the McCloskeys have extremely tidy, coordinated children," said George, "or their kids aren't allowed in the living room. Imagine a white couch in our house."

"It would have been splooched with chocolate and grape juice five minutes after we brought it home," replied Francie, smiling.

George laughed.

Francie looked at her watch.

George refilled their plates and announced that the McCloskeys planned to serve dessert after midnight. "White chocolate mousse. In fancy little individual parfait cups."

Francie looked at her watch again.

"What?" said George. He checked his own watch. "It's only nine thirty. Betsy doesn't have to be home until two."

Francie set her plate aside, crossed her legs, and then crossed them in the other direction. "I know. It's just that . . ." She looked sideways at George.

"Oh no. What? It's just that what?"

"It's just that . . . Don't you think tonight would be a good time for another terrorist attack? Midnight on New Year's Eve?"

George frowned at her. "Everyone thought there would be an attack last year, for Y2K, and nothing happened."

"That was before September eleventh, before the anthrax attacks, too. Things are different now."

"What are you saying?"

"That I want to go home?"

"Right now?"

"Well, before midnight. So we can be with the kids, just in case."

George set his wineglass on the end table with a bit too much force. A tiny Christmas tree that was propped in front of a lamp toppled dangerously, and one miniature glass ornament rolled to the floor. George glanced down at it, then turned back to Francie.

"This is the first time we've been out, just us, in weeks," he said. "And you want to go home early on a night when we have Betsy lined up until two, so we can be with the kids in case terrorists drop a bomb on Vandeventer Avenue?"

Francie looked squarely into George's eyes. "Yes."

At 11:00 when Francie and George had paid Betsy for seven hours of sitting, even though she had gone home three hours early, they sat on their own living room couch, which was protected from chocolate and grape juice with an arrangement of washable towels, and looked at Georgia and Richard, who had fallen asleep on the floor.

"This is so much fun!" said George.

"Don't be sarcastic. It feels safe," replied Francie. She switched on CNN for news of attacks but found nothing except coverage of New Year's celebrations around the world.

George sighed. "Should we put the kids to bed?"

"No. They'd be disappointed. Let's wake them just before midnight."

"Do you think we'll be alive then?"

Francie turned hurt eyes on her husband. "I can't help it!" she cried. "I'm just trying to protect them."

"I'm sorry." George's face softened. He took Francie's hands in his. "Really. I'm sorry. I know you're doing what you think is right."

"All I want is for them to have a nice, peaceful life without so many dangers."

"But, *honey*." George released Francie's hands. "There's no place without *any* dangers."

"I can think of one place with a lot fewer dangers."

"You can?"

Francie nodded. "Lewisport."

"Maine," said George. "The beach cottage."

Francie turned to him, suddenly earnest. "I want us to move there."

George laughed. "You're kidding, right?"

"I'm totally serious."

"Move to the *beach* cottage?"

"Yes."

"*Move* there?"

"Yes."

"You really are serious."

"I really am."

"But what about my job? And the cottage is so small. And . . . and we haven't discussed this. It's coming out of the blue. You always do this, Francie. You throw things at me —"

Across the room, Richard stirred. George lowered his voice. "Do you know what this would mean? What are the job possibilities for me if we move there?"

"You can teach anywhere."

"Lewisport doesn't even have a school."

"There are schools in other towns."

George stood up. He was shaking his head. "Unbelievable."

"I don't see what the problem is."

"The problem is that we have a perfectly nice life here. Our families are nearby. I love my job. We love this house.

The kids love their school. They have friends here. And you're asking us to give all that up because we live too close to Manhattan?"

"Kind of." Francie smiled.

"This isn't funny."

"I know." Francie stood up, crossed the room to Georgia and Richard, and stooped down to touch their cheeks. Then she stood and faced George again. "I can't live here anymore," she told him.

# Chapter 4

*Saturday, October 26th, 2002*

The first thing that sprang into Georgia Noble's mind when she awoke on the Saturday before Halloween was that there was a good chance no one except the people in her own family and her new best friend, Ava, would know what her costume was.

"You want to dress up as *who*?" Richard had asked two weeks earlier, when, over a supper of macaroni and cheese at the little kitchen table in the beach cottage, Georgia had announced her costume decision.

"Buster Brown," she had repeated. "And Henry can be Tige. Okay, Henry?"

"Who's Tige?" Henry wanted to know.

"Good question," said Richard, shaking his head.

"Well, who are *you* going to be?" asked Georgia, glaring at her older brother.

"A zombie. Everyone knows what a zombie is."

"Where on earth did you hear about Buster Brown and Tige?" Georgia's mother asked her daughter.

"From Nana Dana. She said when she was little she had shoes called Buster Browns, and inside there was a picture of a cartoon boy and his dog, Tige."

"Tige is a dog?" said Henry, suddenly interested. "I want to be a dog."

"Thank you," said Georgia. "Anyway, Nana Dana said there was a song about Buster Brown and Tige. It went, 'Does your shoe have a boy inside?' and then 'Does your shoe have a dog there, too?' The song went on and on. We looked on the computer and Nana Dana showed me a picture of Buster Brown and Tige. And that's who I think Henry and I should be for Halloween."

"Well, that's certainly a very creative choice," her father had commented.

But now, on the day of Lewisport's Halloween celebration, Georgia began to question her decision.

"Maybe one of the judges will be really old," Richard had said the day before. "You know, like in his fifties. Like Nana Dana. And he'll know who Buster Brown and Tige are. Besides, you made good costumes."

Georgia had basked in this rare compliment from her

brother and had felt a bit better. Now she sat up in her bed and listened for early morning sounds in the beach cottage.

"We really must stop calling it the beach cottage," her mother kept saying. "This is our home now, not a temporary vacation place."

It felt temporary, though, even after their furniture from New Jersey had arrived. Not that there was room for much of the furniture. The house in Princeton had been several times the size of the cottage. Most of their furniture had been sold along with the rambling house on Vandeventer Avenue. Georgia had been surprised when her mother had announced that they were moving, but not saddened. She loved the cottage and Lewisport and frankly didn't care whether she went to school in New Jersey or in Maine. Leslie had already moved away. In February, Mrs. Jordan had packed up the house and driven Leslie and her brother right out of Princeton and all the way to Colorado for a fresh start.

In June, just after school ended, the Nobles had left Princeton, too. Georgia knew that her father had not wanted to move. He had said that finding a teaching job in nearby Barnegat Point, where the kids from teeny Lewisport went to school, would be difficult, and he'd been right. September had rolled around, school had started, and Georgia's father had no job. Maybe, Georgia thought, this was one reason the house still felt like a temporary place. Sure, her bed and dresser from her room on Vandeventer Avenue were set up in her room at the cottage. Sure, the Nobles had been living there for four months. Sure, Georgia and Richard were enrolled at Barnegat Point Elementary — the very same school her great-grandma Abby had once attended. But coming home from school every day to a house on the beach — and to a father who was hanging around in his jeans and a T-shirt — felt like vacation.

Georgia peered behind the blinds at the yard outside her window. Her room at the back of the house had been added on ten years earlier, so there were now two bedrooms downstairs. A second bathroom had been added at the same time, this one off the upstairs bedroom. The cottage, Georgia felt, fit her family just fine. Although as Richard frequently pointed out, Georgia did not have to share her room with anyone. She had a room to herself while he had to share with Henry, *who was such a baby.*

Georgia had just let the blinds fall back into place when she heard a rattling at her window. She pulled the blinds aside again and found herself facing a small fierce girl whose dark hair had been woven in two neat braids, tied with purple ribbons.

"Ava!" she cried softly.

Her best friend, Ava Norwood, grinned at her. "Get up! It's almost six thirty. You don't want to waste Saturday, do you?"

Georgia did not want to waste Saturday. Saturdays on Blue Harbor Lane were much more interesting than Saturdays on Vandeventer Avenue. There was the ocean, for one thing, although at this time of year it was too cold to swim in. But that didn't mean she and Ava couldn't comb the sand for shells and pebbles to turn into jewelry.

"We could become millionaires!" Ava had proclaimed when Georgia had shared her great idea.

Georgia felt as if she had fit right into life in tiny Lewisport, belonging in the town as surely as if she'd been born there, as Ava had. She and Richard and Henry had been swallowed up by the gang of Blue Harbor Lane kids almost as soon as their car had pulled into the driveway. All day long they wandered up and down the short street, running in and out of one another's houses, playing basketball and soccer, a noisy, sweaty bunch, until daylight faded and parents started calling the kids inside for baths and bed. The adults' sole rule was that the kids — all of them — were forbidden to cross the street and venture onto the beach without a grown-up.

To Georgia's amazement, her mother — the same mother who hadn't allowed her to go unaccompanied next door to

Leslie's house in Princeton — now seemed perfectly comfortable allowing her and Richard to roam the street, and beyond. "It's safe here," she'd said, looking fondly up and down the sunny strip of road. "A safe little world."

All the Blue Harbor Lane kids regularly walked to the end of the spit of land on which Lewisport sat and around the bend to what they called "town."

"When your great-grandma Abby was growing up here," Georgia's mother often said, "there was no town. Just a store."

"*One* store?" Georgia liked to say.

"One store. A general store. You could buy everything there from flour to toys to underwear."

"Underpants?" Henry would shriek.

"Yes, underpants. And almost anything else you could think of."

"Which store was it?" Georgia had asked once.

Her mother had shaken her head. "It's gone. Long gone. But it was where the coffee shop is now."

Georgia had a hard time imagining one lonely store on the street that was now lined with two small markets, a post office, a pharmacy, a stationery store, a doctor's office, an ice-cream shop, a bicycle repair shop, a bookstore, a church, a gas station, a shoe store, and several businesses that Georgia found quite boring, such as a Laundromat and a bank. There was also a tattoo parlor — a source of great fascination — but that was where her mother had put her foot down. No child of hers was allowed in a tattoo parlor. Georgia didn't care. She could go off with the other kids and roam to her heart's content, as long as she checked in with her parents from time to time and didn't stray from Blue Harbor Lane and the street through town.

All summer long, Georgia and Ava, often joined by Penny and Talia, sisters who lived at one end of the lane, had entertained themselves busily. When they'd tired of basketball and soccer they'd raided the library in Barnegat Point for books about time travel and wizardry, which they read in a fort behind Ava's house. They had taken diving lessons at the Y and then tap lessons at Miss Tabby's Dance Studio. And they had begun their jewelry business, which so far had netted them nearly three and a half dollars apiece.

It was when the girls were waiting to be picked up after their diving lesson one afternoon that Georgia had heard the sound of a music class in progress. She had peeped through a partially open door at the end of a hall and seen a boy strumming a guitar.

"That's what I want to do," she had informed her friends. "I want to play the guitar."

Three weeks later she'd found herself sitting not in a class at the Y, but in the living room of a man named Mr. Elden, who gave private guitar lessons.

"He's the best music teacher in the area," Ava's mother had told the Nobles. "He teaches at the elementary school, too."

By September, Georgia had her own secondhand guitar, and it had become part of her life.

"I just wish," her mother had said more than once, "that Mr. Elden didn't give lessons in his *house*. I'd feel much more comfortable if Georgia's lessons were at the school."

"But I love Mr. Elden!" Georgia had cried.

Her father had said, "Mr. Elden teaches kids from all over the county. We're lucky he took Georgia on."

That was the end of the discussion.

Now on this October Saturday, the day of the Halloween celebration, Georgia thought of the lovely hours stretching ahead of her. She invited Ava inside, and they ate donuts and examined the Buster Brown and Tige costumes while the rest of the Nobles slowly awoke. They spent the morning with Penny and Talia, ate lunch at Ava's house, asked Ava's father to accompany them to the beach so they could find shells for their jewelry, and finally returned to Georgia's house to look at the costumes one last time.

"What do we get if we win the costume contest?" Henry asked Ava.

Georgia was adjusting Tige's paws.

"Nothing," Ava replied. "One of the judges just says, 'And the winner is' and then everybody gets to hear your name."

"Huh," said Henry. "Okay."

"Kids!" called Georgia's mother, and Georgia peeked into the living room where Mrs. Noble had set up her computer and was trying to write her next book — but having very little success. ("I hit a dry spell," Georgia overheard her say to Ava's mother.)

"Yes?" said Georgia and her brothers.

"Great-Grandma and Orrin will be here soon. Time to get ready to go to the community center."

Ava jumped to her feet. "See you later!" she called.

Great-Grandma and Orrin arrived later in their ancient black car, the one that Georgia's father sometimes called the Gas Guzzler and sometimes called the Behemoth.

Georgia met them at the door. "Great-Grandma!" she cried, and wrapped her arms around the woman named Abigail Cora who had been born in this very house and who had grown up here, too. Georgia liked to imagine the women in her family as a set of nesting dolls. The outer doll, Great-Grandma, sheltering her daughter Dana, who sheltered her daughter, Francie, who sheltered the innermost doll, the tiny and whole Georgia Eleanor Goldberg Noble.

"Hello, lovey," said Great-Grandma. She shrugged out of her wool coat, which she handed to Orrin. Orrin was Great-Grandma's husband, but not the father of her children. He was her second husband.

"Orrin was the boy you used to play with when you were little?" Georgia had asked Great-Grandma at least a hundred times. "The one you fell in love with when you were in second grade?"

"The very one," Great-Grandma would reply, and she would tell Georgia stories about growing up on Blue Harbor Lane, of clamming and blueberry-picking with little Orrin Umhay in a time Georgia had difficulty imagining.

Great-Grandma and Orrin sat on the couch by the front door and held hands while Georgia and Richard and Henry gave them a preview of their costumes.

"A zombie. Very scary," said Orrin seriously when Richard marched into the room.

But when Georgia and Henry emerged from Georgia's bedroom, Great-Grandma put her hand to her mouth and exclaimed, "Well, I'll be! Buster Brown and Tige! I haven't thought about them in years."

Georgia shot Richard a look that plainly said, "See? Great-Grandma knows who I am." Richard pretended not to see her.

Finally Georgia's father said, "All right, everybody. Let's get a move on."

"Do we get to ride in the Behemoth tonight?" asked Richard with great excitement.

"There aren't enough seat belts," said Georgia's mother. "Great-Grandma and Orrin will come in the van with us."

They pulled out onto Blue Harbor Lane, four adults, Buster Brown, Tige, and a zombie.

The community center was crowded. Georgia saw her Blue Harbor Lane friends and their families, her second-grade teacher, Richard's third-grade teacher, three of Henry's preschool classmates, the owner of the gas station, the owners of the coffee shop, and Mr. Elden. She took Great-Grandma's hand and they walked all around the room, exclaiming over the glowing pumpkins and wobbly scarecrows, sampling candy and cider, and trying their hands at the ring toss and penny pitch.

"This reminds me of the carnivals my sister Rose and I used to go to when were little," said Great-Grandma.

"Did Orrin go, too?" asked Georgia. She glanced across

the room at Orrin, who was giving Richard tips on the penny pitch.

"Sometimes. His family didn't have much money, though." She paused. "Of course, neither did mine."

Again Georgia cast her mind back to Great-Grandma's childhood days, the ones that seemed impossibly far away. She wondered if, when she was Great-Grandma's age, this moment at the Halloween celebration would seem just as far away, or if it would be something she would remember clearly but would seem foreign to her own great-granddaughter.

Georgia was still mulling over these questions of time when Mrs. Dean, the principal, announced that the parade would begin. Buster Brown, Tige, and dozens of other costumed Lewisport children walked slowly around the room while their parents and families and friends applauded.

In the end, the panel of judges, some older and some younger, announced that the winner was a girl dressed as a teacup, which Georgia had to admit was an original idea. She had no idea whether anyone had recognized her or Henry, but she didn't care. She stood among Ava and her great-grandma and Orrin and Mr. Elden and Penny and Talia, her hands sticky with candy corn, and decided this was the nicest Halloween she could remember.

# Chapter 5

"Georgia! Georgia! Wake up! It's pageant day!"

Georgia came to with a jolt as Henry burst through her door and sprang onto the foot of her bed. He jumped up and down, bare feet jostling her collection of stuffed animals, as well as Noelle.

"Henry, be careful!" exclaimed Georgia, sitting up and rescuing Noelle from where she'd been snoozing between a teddy bear wearing glasses and a garish purple turtle.

"Sorry, Noelle," said Henry contritely. He sat down and took the kitten from Georgia, pulling her into his lap. Then he exclaimed, "But it's pageant day!"

"I know." Georgia smiled.

"Aren't you excited?"

"Of course I am. Is Richard awake yet?"

Henry shook his head. "But I'm awake and I'm excited!"

There were still five days until Christmas, but today was going to be almost as good as Christmas itself.

"What time are Great-Grandma and Orrin coming?" Henry wanted to know. Ever since he'd started kindergarten he had asked this question frequently, mostly to demonstrate that he was learning to tell time.

"Five o'clock, I think." Georgia took Noelle from her brother and held her in her lap, stroking her silky gray fur. She wished Nana Dana would visit at Christmas, too — would make the trip to Lewisport from her apartment in New York City — but her grandmother rarely visited Maine. Something to do with Great-Grandma, Georgia had deduced. No one would talk about whatever was wrong between Great-Grandma and Nana Dana, but there was something, something Georgia didn't understand.

"I can't wait until five o'clock!" cried Henry.

"You have to. Besides, we have a lot to do today."

Henry eyed her suspiciously. "We don't have to help at Daddy's store, do we?"

"Nope." Georgia knew that the Saturday before Christmas would be a big shopping day. The store her father had opened the previous spring, A Doll's House, had gotten off to a slow start, but Mr. Noble kept saying, "The tourists will carry us through." The tourists had arrived on Memorial Day and left by Labor Day and still the shop, which sold dollhouses and dollhouse dolls and furniture (and nothing else) was limping along. So Georgia's father had set his hopes on holiday shoppers. Richard, Georgia, and even Henry (Mrs. Noble, too, when she wasn't writing) had sometimes been drafted to help in the store, since Mr. Noble couldn't afford to pay a clerk. But he had assured his children that today, the day of the pageant, they were off the hook.

"Come on. Let's look at the Christmas tree," Georgia whispered to her brother. "But be quiet, because everyone else is still asleep."

They tiptoed to her doorway and looked at the tree in the corner of the living room. They had decorated it the night before and now the ornaments twinkled in the faint glow of the rising sun.

"Turn on the lights!" Henry begged.

Georgia plugged in the lights and the tree shimmered softly.

"Maybe it will snow," said Henry hopefully, peering across Blue Harbor Lane at the snow-free beach and the brightening sky.

Georgia had checked the Weather Channel the night before. She knew there wasn't any snow in the forecast. "We'd better write our letters to Santa this afternoon," she said brightly. "Plus, we have to practice for the pageant."

Just like that, Henry turned his attention away from snow.

\* \* \*

After breakfast that morning, Georgia retreated to her room and closed her door. She took her guitar from its case and sat on the edge of her bed. Her lessons with Mr. Elden were progressing well — she now took lessons at school in addition to private lessons — and when her Sunday school teacher at the Presbyterian church had begun planning the pageant, Georgia had been asked not to play a sheep or an angel, but to provide the background for the carols that would be sung.

Georgia's mother had smiled when she'd seen the music for the pageant. "You know, I grew up celebrating the Jewish holidays with Papa Matthew, and only going to church with Nana Dana sometimes."

"Why?" Georgia had asked. Before her mother could answer, she had added, "Am I Jewish, too?"

"You are one quarter Jewish," was the reply. "You're one quarter African American, too."

Georgia had nodded. She knew that her great-grandparents, her father's mother's parents, were black. But she hadn't given it much thought. Now she did the math. "I'm one quarter Jewish and one quarter black and three quarters not Jewish and three quarters not black. How come that adds up to more than one?"

Her mother had laughed. "It does add up to one. It adds up to one whole Georgia Eleanor Goldberg Noble."

Georgia studied her music and then played through the songs for the pageant. She played them again and decided she knew them well — very well. She didn't know them perfectly, but she had realized not long after starting her lessons with Mr. Elden that there was no such thing as perfection in music anyway. Georgia was satisfied with the performance she would give that night.

She gathered the music into a folder and pulled her guitar onto her lap again. She had thought long and hard about a Christmas gift for her parents that year and, almost without realizing what she was doing, had eventually begun to compose a song for them. She played it softly now and was halfway through when she was interrupted by a knock on her door.

"Come in," she said.

Richard and Henry entered the room, Richard dressed as a Wise Man, Henry as a lamb.

"How do we look?" asked Henry.

"Great. Your costumes are really good."

Richard slumped on the bed, his cardboard crown sliding off of his head. "Can I borrow some money? I don't have a present for Mom and Dad yet."

Georgia shook her head. "I haven't got a cent."

"What happened to all that money you made selling jewelry?"

"Selling jewelry?! That was last year, in second grade."

"Well, don't you have any more?"

Allowances in the Noble household had been cut months ago.

"No. What happened to your money?"

Richard shrugged. "Spent it." He was no good at thinking ahead. "Hey, if you don't have any money, how are *you* going to get a present for Mom and Dad?"

Georgia smiled. "None of your business." She purposely kept her eyes from straying to her guitar. She had no intention of spoiling the surprise. This was the best gift she had ever thought of.

Henry, the Velcro on his hoofs coming unfastened so that his lamb feet separated from his lamb body, said earnestly, "We made presents for our parents in school."

"Really?" said Richard. "What did you make? Hand prints?"

"*No,*" Henry replied, sounding insulted. "I made a macaroni chain for our Christmas tree."

Georgia saw the look on Richard's face and stepped in hastily. "You know what Henry and I decided this morning?"

she said. "We decided that we'd better write our letters to Santa. Let's do that now, okay? You guys take off your costumes. We'll write the letters at the kitchen table."

Georgia tiptoed through the living room, where her mother sat in front of her computer, working away. She had a deadline, Georgia knew, which meant that she had a book due, and if her mother had a book due, then a check would be arriving in the mail soon. That was a good thing, considering the conversation Georgia had tried not to overhear the night before. The conversation, drifting down from her parents' upstairs bedroom, had begun with her father saying that in the previous week the store had *almost* broken even, and ended with her mother saying that if the store continued to lose money she insisted they shut it down.

This morning her parents hadn't spoken a word to each other before Mr. Noble had left the cottage to walk to work.

Georgia assembled paper and markers on the table and waited for her brothers. Eventually, they entered the kitchen, costume-free, Henry nearly vibrating with excitement. Before he even sat down he announced, "What I want is a dog and an emerald."

"What do you want an emerald for?" Richard asked as he settled himself in his chair. He didn't sound scornful, just curious.

Henry shrugged. "To be rich. If you have an emerald you must be rich."

"Good thinking!" said Georgia. "Okay, let's get started. Henry, do you need help or do you want to spell everything yourself?"

"Myself," her brother replied, reaching for a red marker.

They worked busily. Georgia composed a letter following the guidelines she was learning in school. She began with a greeting; inquired after the health of Santa, his wife, the elves, and the reindeer; filled Santa in on her life that year; asked for three books and a Nintendo; and finished with a thank-you and a formal closing.

"All done!" Henry announced as Georgia was signing her name to her letter. "Look."

He held out his letter, which read: *DER SANTE, THAT YOU AND MURY CRISMIS. PLES I WOD LIKE A EMREAL IF YOU HAV ONE IN YUR SLA. PLUS A DOG. PLUS A JEEP. FROM HENRY NOBLE.*

"Let's mail them right now!" said Henry. "Please?"

Georgia and Richard automatically glanced into the living room at their mother. Mailing letters to Santa involved the use of the fireplace, and therefore required an adult.

"Mom's busy," Richard whispered to Georgia.

"I know, but I think she'll help us."

She did. Their mom seemed glad to take a break. She let Richard light the fire that had been laid in the hearth, and then one by one, she held the Santa letters lightly above the flames and allowed them to be carried up the chimney.

"All right. Back to work," she said, smiling.

Henry turned to Georgia and whispered, "Let's go outside and look for them."

Georgia and her brothers put their jackets on and ran outdoors.

"Where are they?" cried Henry, his head tipped back. "I don't see any letters in the air."

"Probably at the North Pole," Richard replied.

"No, it's too soon. They couldn't have gotten all the way to the North Pole already!" Henry dashed through the backyard and along a path that was a shortcut into town. Soon he veered off the path, Georgia and Richard at his heels, his face turned to the sunny sky.

Henry ran and ran, and Georgia and Richard ran after him. By the time they returned to the cottage, Henry tearful because the letters had not been spotted, they were met at the door by their angry mother.

"Where on earth were you? I didn't hear you leave the house. Ava stopped by looking for you, Georgia, and I didn't even know you were gone." She paused to take a breath.

"Great-Grandma and Orrin will be here soon, and your father's on his way home. Go get ready for the pageant."

"Sorry, sorry," said Georgia breathlessly. "Henry wanted to see our letters in the sky."

"And we couldn't," he added, bursting into fresh tears.

Their mother sat on the couch, her eyes softening. "I'm sure your letters have reached Santa by now," she said. "Truly. It's all magic, remember? Now, scoot. Go get your costumes."

Not long after darkness had fallen that night, Georgia paused before the Presbyterian church at the edge of Lewisport. The stained-glass windows glowed crimson and violet and indigo blue, and the front doors stood open, spilling light into the hushed yard. Georgia, her guitar slung over one shoulder, held tight to Great-Grandma's hand and looked around at her family — her parents, who, she was relieved to see, were also holding hands; Orrin, his arm across Richard's shoulder; and Henry, who was singing "Away in a Manger" so softly that his voice was like a gull feather in the night air.

Georgia tipped her face up and looked at her great-grandmother. "Did you go to this church when you were little?" she asked.

"Sometimes. It wasn't our church, but sometimes I came here with my friend Sarah." Great-Grandma's eyes strayed to the tiny cemetery enclosed by a stone wall. Her chin quivered just slightly. "Well," she said at last. "Well."

"Come on. Let's *go!*" cried Henry.

Georgia squeezed Great-Grandma's hand and she and her family climbed the steps to the open doors just as the organ came to life and the first notes of "Silent Night" reached Georgia's ears.

# Chapter 6

*Thursday, August 5th, 2004*

Georgia, Ava, Penny, and Talia sat in a row on the top step of Georgia's tiny front porch. Henry sat below them, on the bottom step, his face turned so that he could look up at them, one hand shielding his eyes from the blazing sun.

"What should we do now?" asked Talia.

"Yeah, what should we do?" echoed Henry.

"It's too hot to do anything," Ava replied. "Too hot to do anything at all."

The August sun beat down on them. Summers in Maine weren't usually hot, at least not this hot, and the afternoon stretched stickily ahead of them.

"Let's go to the library," suggested Penny. "It's air-conditioned."

"I don't feel like the library," said Talia.

The Blue Harbor Lane kids had spent the morning playing Forensic Detectives. (Henry had twice asked what this meant, hadn't understood either explanation, and had renamed the game Forever Detectives.) Eleven children had crept from house to house, tiptoed inside each one undetected (they hoped), and gathered hair from combs and made off with mugs containing cold swigs of coffee. They had analyzed their evidence in Ava's backyard using a fingerprint kit and Penny and Talia's grandmother's reading glasses.

"Whoever drank from this mug," Richard had announced at last, "is definitely a criminal."

"That's Mom's mug!" cried Henry.

Richard swatted his brother's head. "Pretend!"

"Use your imagination!" Talia had added.

The game had continued as the heat had risen. One by one, the children had drifted away. Richard and his friends Austin and Alex had retreated to Austin's air-conditioned house with a stack of comic books. The Quigley boys (twins named Doug and Sandy, but everyone called them simply "the Quigley boys") had gone home to beg someone to take them across the street to the beach.

For a while, Georgia had sat alone on her stoop while Henry played inside with Noelle. She watched the waves washing onto the beach and thought about fourth grade, which would start in a month. Then she thought about her lessons with Mr. Elden and how he had said she would probably need a new guitar soon. After that, her thoughts turned to A Doll's House. The store was still in business, but just barely. It was still only limping along.

"How long are we going to hang on to something that doesn't turn a profit?" Georgia's mother had asked her father after a disappointing Memorial Day weekend when Mr. Noble had sold exactly one dollhouse, one dollhouse family, and twelve pieces of dollhouse furniture.

"Just give me the rest of the tourist season," he'd replied. "Let's make a decision in September."

They were now closer to September than to Memorial Day, and not much had changed.

"Georgie Girl, lunch," said a voice behind her, and Georgia had jumped.

"Sorry, honey, I didn't mean to startle you." Her mother stood in the doorway, cell phone in hand. "Where's Richard?" she'd asked.

"At Austin's."

Fifteen minutes later, Georgia, Richard, Henry, and their mother were seated around their kitchen table eating sandwiches and grapes. Georgia swung her sandy feet back and forth and gazed into the living room at her mother's worktable. It was littered with papers and books. She could see the blinking light that meant the computer had gone to sleep. Her mother was deeply involved in another book, this one her very first mystery.

"I could help you with your book," Richard said, setting down his sandwich. "I could do forensic research for you."

"Thank you," said Mrs. Noble, smiling. "I appreciate it, but —"

"Mom, how did you become a criminal?" asked Henry.

"What?" Mrs. Noble frowned at him, then began to laugh. "Where did you —" Her phone rang then and she looked at the caller ID. "Sorry, guys," she said. "I have to take this. It's my editor. You finish up here and then let me work until dinnertime, okay? I have a deadline. Georgia, remember your lesson with Mr. Elden this afternoon. Two o'clock. When you're at home, you're in charge of Henry. Richard, you're in charge of both of them," she added hastily.

Mrs. Noble left her half-eaten sandwich and sat down at her computer. Five minutes later, Georgia and her brothers had finished their lunches and cleared the table. Richard dashed out the front door.

"Where are you going?" Georgia called after him.

"Don't know."

"Well, come back at quarter to two and get Henry, okay? He's your responsibility while I'm at my lesson."

"Okay," Richard shouted over his shoulder. The screen door banged shut behind him.

This was when Georgia and Henry had sat out on their front stoop in the sticky heat.

"What are we doing?" Henry had asked.

"Waiting for something to happen."

What had happened was that Ava, Penny, and Talia had shown up, Penny had suggested going to the library, and Talia had rejected the notion.

"Then what should we *do*?" whined Penny.

"Let's make an outfit for Noelle," said Ava.

"No, she hates wearing clothes," said Georgia. "Besides, Mom says it isn't fair to make animals wear clothes."

Talia stretched her brown legs in front of her. "This is the most bored I've ever been."

Georgia looked at her watch. "I have a lesson in twenty minutes," she announced. "Richard had better come back soon. He promised he would." She stood up. "I have to get my stuff ready."

"Okay. See you later," said Ava, and she and Penny and Talia wandered off, still complaining of boredom.

"Can I go with you?" Henry asked his sister.

"What? To Mr. Elden's?" (He nodded.) "Sure. I guess so. Just remember that you have to be quiet during the lesson, okay?"

"Okay." Almost everything was okay with Henry.

Richard returned at the last possible moment, and Georgia told him that she was taking Henry along for her lesson.

"Excellent!" said Richard.

"We'll be back in an hour," she added, as Richard ran jubilantly down Blue Harbor Lane to rejoin his friends.

They were back in one hour and five minutes.

"That was really fun," Henry was saying as they approached the cottage, even though he had done nothing but listen to his sister's lesson. "Someday maybe I'll —"

The door of the cottage blasted open and Mrs. Noble appeared on the front steps, cell phone in hand. "Oh, thank *goodness!*" she exclaimed, although she looked angry, rather than relieved. "There you are." She paused. "Where *were* you?"

Georgia frowned. She pointed to her guitar. "At my lesson. Remember?"

"I know where *you* were, but where has Henry been? I've been looking and looking for him. The Quigley boys came by asking for him, and I said he must be with Richard and they said he wasn't, that Richard had gone off with Austin and Alex. Then I began calling the neighbors, and Ava said she thought Henry was with Richard, too, which by then I knew wasn't true. No one knew where he was. No one had seen him. And I remembered a strange car I saw down the street this morning."

Georgia stepped forward. "Mom. It's okay. Henry was with me. He wanted to go to my lesson. He's right here. See? He's fine."

"Well, why didn't you tell me he was going with you? I was *this* close to calling the police," Mrs. Noble went on, and Georgia heard a tremor in her voice. "*This* close, Georgia. You know better."

"Hey, this isn't my fault!" she cried. She stepped around her mother and entered the cottage, slinging her guitar onto the living room couch. "You said not to bother you this afternoon, so I didn't. But I did tell Richard where we were going. And you knew I was going to my lesson."

"But I didn't know you were taking Henry with you."

"But I *told Richard*. You said Richard was in charge of Henry and me."

"Well, Richard didn't tell me."

Georgia's heart, which had begun pounding, began to slow down. She drew in a deep breath. "I'm sorry, Mom.

I'm sorry Richard didn't tell you what we were doing. We didn't mean to scare you." Then she added, "It really wasn't my fault. Anyway, nothing is wrong. Henry's here and he's okay."

Henry had sat down on the couch with the guitar. His lip was quivering. "Sorry, Mom," he said.

Mrs. Noble sat next to him, but Georgia remained standing. "You act like this is my fault," she said, voice rising. "And you *said* Richard was in charge of —"

"I know what I said, but you were irresponsible."

"You *told* us not to *bother* you!"

"You could have left a note. That's the least you could have done."

"Why is this my fault?" Georgia demanded. "I don't understand." Despite herself, she stamped her foot. She stamped it so hard that the floor shook and Noelle fled from the room.

Her mother looked pointedly from Noelle's disappearing tail to Georgia's stormy face. Then she said, "You were the one who took Henry to your lesson."

"So?"

"So, you kids have plenty of independence here, but you have to earn it. It isn't a privilege. No one knew where Henry was this afternoon, and that's unacceptable."

"*I* knew where he was!" Georgia exploded. "And so did Richard."

"So did I," said Henry in a small voice.

Georgia smiled, but her mother shook her head. "This isn't a joke. No one told me about the change in plans and nobody I spoke to knew where Henry was. Georgia, your punishment is that you can't play with Ava for a week."

"What?!"

"You heard me. That's the end of the discussion. Go to your room until dinnertime."

Georgia marched into her room and slammed the door behind her. "It was just a mistake!" she shouted. "It was a misunderstanding. Just because I'm the responsible one, I'm the one who gets punished! You expect more from me. You never punish Richard, but you punish me all the time. I'm the one who gets the good grades, I'm the one who cleans my room and does my chores and practices my guitar. I do everything right, and then when the littlest thing goes wrong, *I* get punished. It isn't fair." Georgia held her ear to her door and listened for sounds from the living room. When she heard only the clacking of the keys on her mother's laptop, she shouted again, *"It isn't fair!"*

# Chapter 7

*Saturday, March 19th, 2005*

Georgia rolled over in the unfamiliar bed in the unfamiliar room. The first thing she saw was her mother sleeping in a matching bed beside her. She tiptoed to the window, quietly raised the venetian blind, and blinked in the sunlight. Below her was the world of West 73rd Street in Manhattan. She knew that if she could crane her head far enough to the right she'd be able to see West End Avenue. Georgia peeked at her watch. Seven thirty. Seven thirty on a Saturday morning and already the city was busy. Taxis glided by. A man hurried along walking three tiny white dogs on leashes that glittered. Each dog carried a toy in its mouth, and the man carried a brown paper bag in his free hand. A woman pushed a stroller with two screaming children in it. Even from the fourth floor Georgia could hear their shrieks. The woman checked her cell phone and ignored the noise.

Georgia turned from the window and crept back to her bed. She lay there, smiling, recalling the events — they still seemed surreal to her — that had brought her to Nana Dana's apartment for a weekend in Manhattan, and what she hoped was the beginning of her professional music career.

Her adventure had begun just over a month earlier when, at the end of band practice at Barnegat Point Elementary one afternoon, Mr. Elden had crooked his finger at Georgia and said, "Could you stay for a few minutes, please? I need to talk to you about something."

Ava, who played keyboard in the band, had raised her eyebrows at Georgia and whispered ever so softly, "Woo-hoo." All the students at BP Elementary thought Mr. Elden was cool, even though he was middle-aged — older than Georgia's own parents — and his hair was turning gray.

"Have you ever seen him perform?" Talia had asked Georgia one day. "He plays guitar in a band on weekends. Like in restaurants and clubs and stuff. He plays *electric* guitar. He looks like a TV star then, not like a teacher." She had added rapturously, as most of the girls did when the subject of Mr. Elden came up, "He is SO AWESOME."

Georgia hadn't seen him play except when he was giving lessons, but she agreed that he was awesome. Now, as he motioned to her to stay behind after class, Georgia flashed Ava a self-conscious smile and returned to her seat.

"So," said Mr. Elden, when the room had emptied. He perched on his desk in the cramped practice space. "I have an opportunity for you."

Georgia looked at him with interest. "An opportunity?"

"I have a friend in the business —" He noticed the confusion on Georgia's face and said, "The music business. He's based in New York and he's looking for a kid to perform in a piece to promote a music video."

"Yes?" said Georgia, willing herself not to get too excited.

"I thought of you right away. You're my most talented guitar student. You play way beyond your level, and you're already creating your own style. Would you be interested in performing in the video? The piece will be very short, but it would be nice exposure for you."

Georgia could contain herself no longer. She jumped out of her chair. "Yes! Yes, I would love that! It would be so exciting!"

Mr. Elden grinned. "Excellent. I hoped that would be your response. A few things, though. We'll need to send Joe — he's my friend — some footage of you playing your guitar. We'll need to put together something that will show off your strengths and your range. Also, the piece is going to be shot in New York City, so you and I and one of your parents will have to travel there."

Georgia had begun babbling then — about her dream of becoming a professional guitar player, about Nana Dana and her apartment in Manhattan, and about how this opportunity was a dream come true. What she didn't say was that she couldn't imagine her mother okaying a trip to NYC with Mr. Elden.

Mr. Elden put out a hand to slow her down. "Go home, talk to your parents, and then ask one of them to call me. We'll take it from there."

At home that evening, Georgia had waited until her house was quiet and homework time was underway (although Richard, she knew, was under his covers with his Nintendo, not his math book).

"Mom? Dad?" said Georgia, standing uncertainly in the living room where her parents were huddled over bank statements and record books. Her father was still the owner of A Doll's House, since the store had picked up slightly — ever so slightly — by the end of the previous summer, but the holidays had been disastrous. "Can I talk to you?"

"Sure. What's up, Georgie Girl?" her father replied vaguely.

"It's sort of important."

Her parents put the papers away and gave Georgia their full attention. She sat across from them and reported everything that Mr. Elden had told her. She tried to sound serious and grown-up.

Mr. Noble's eyes had brightened and he'd taken his daughter's hand and exclaimed, "Honey, that's wonderful! This really is an opportunity. I'll call Mr. Elden right away."

But Mrs. Noble had grown serious. She pursed her lips together, threw her husband a venomous look, and said, "Sorry, Georgia, but that's out of the question."

"Mom, please, I really want to go. And Dad agreed that this is an opportunity."

"But a trip to *New York*? To be filmed by some music business person we don't even know?"

"We could stay at Nana Dana's," said Georgia. "We've done that before. We'd be safe there. And Nana Dana could spend the day with us. She wouldn't let anything happen. We'd be safe. *Please.*"

Her mom shook her head. "Out of the question."

But Georgia's father got to his feet. "I'm sorry. Not this time."

Georgia and her mother both looked up at him in confusion.

Mr. Noble turned to his wife. "You are not making this decision by yourself. You do not have the only say in the matter. There are three of us here, and we all get a vote. This is important to Georgia, and she's being very mature about it. I vote that Georgia be allowed to take the opportunity. Georgia?"

"I vote yes, too," said Georgia, practically holding her breath.

"Well, I vote no," said her mother. "But I guess that doesn't matter."

Georgia had thrown her arms around her father. "Oh, thank you, thank you, thank you!" she'd cried. "You know, I still might not get to go. I still have to send in a DVD, but thank you for saying I can try."

Georgia had gotten to go, of course. It hadn't been easy. Putting together a DVD that showed off all the skills Mr. Elden thought were important, as well as her technique and style, was far more complicated and time-consuming than Georgia had imagined it would be. She'd worked hard, though, both at home on her own and during her lessons with Mr. Elden. Within an hour of viewing the DVD, Mr. Elden's friend had announced that he wanted Georgia for the video.

And so the planning had begun. After much discussion among the adults, including Nana Dana in New York, it was decided that Georgia and her mother would go to Manhattan for a girls' weekend with Nana Dana. The "shoot," as Georgia had learned the filming of the video was called, would take place on a Saturday afternoon. Georgia, Mrs. Noble, and Mr. Elden would leave for New York on Friday. ("You mean she gets a day off *school*?" Richard had exclaimed, incensed.) They would return on Sunday.

"Let's just hope we're all in one piece," Mrs. Noble said more than once.

Now it was Saturday morning, the day of the shoot. Georgia glanced at her mother, who was still asleep, crept into the hallway of Nana Dana's apartment, and tiptoed into the living room.

"Hi, pumpkin," said Nana Dana. She was sitting on the couch with a cup of coffee, which she set down. She opened her arms and Georgia settled into them.

"I saw a man walking three dogs on sparkle leashes," Georgia said into her grandmother's shoulder. Then she added, "Mom is still asleep."

Nana Dana held Georgia at arm's length. "So? Are you excited?"

Georgia nodded. "About the video and also just about being here."

"In New York?"

"In New York with you."

Nana Dana smiled. "When your mother was little she used to love visiting New York."

Georgia widened her eyes. "Really? She did?" She couldn't imagine her mother loving trips to the big bad city.

"Really and truly. She and her father and I would come here for weekends to visit my aunt Adele and your mother would stay with Adele in her apartment. We would go to shows and out to dinner and walk all over the city."

"I wish I lived closer to you," said Georgia, "so we could do things like that."

"Me, too, pumpkin." Nana Dana drew Georgia in for another hug.

At exactly noon, Georgia, her mother, and Nana Dana met Mr. Elden at the entrance to Central Park. With Mr. Elden was a tall man wearing jeans and a leather jacket. The eyes behind his thick black glasses looked stern, but when Mr. Elden said, "Joe, this is Georgia, our star guitar player," Joe smiled warmly.

"Let's get to work," he said.

With Joe were two men lugging cameras, microphones, and all sorts of equipment stored in heavy black cases that they toted much more cheerfully than Georgia would have.

"First," Joe said to Georgia, "we want to shoot you" ("Shoot me?!" Georgia couldn't help thinking) "walking through the park playing your guitar."

Georgia hadn't expected this. She was used to sitting and playing, or occasionally standing and playing. But she gamely slung her guitar strap over her shoulder and, following Joe's directions, began walking along a path in the park, playing "Yesterday" by the Beatles. She was acutely aware of the stares of passersby. It was a chilly, bright Saturday, and even though the weather couldn't be described as springlike, the park was a lively place. Vendors sold hot pretzels and sodas. Children flew along the paths on Rollerblades and scooters, their nervous parents running after them. A karate class was in progress on the lawn. But as Georgia strummed her way through the park — surrounded by Joe and his crew, Mr. Elden, her mother, and Nana Dana — everyone stopped to watch her. She tried to smile at them as she played. She had a feeling she was grimacing instead, but when she glanced self-consciously at Joe, he simply motioned to her to keep going.

After forty-five minutes of walking and playing, Joe finally said, "Okay, that's good! Now we're going to move on to Times Square."

Georgia turned to her mother, astounded, and whispered, "I thought we were done!"

They were far from done. "We need lots of footage," Joe explained.

"How long is the video going to be?" asked Georgia.

"Five minutes."

"Five *minutes*?!"

Joe laughed. "Welcome to show business. You can shoot for hours just to get five minutes of screen time."

After playing her guitar in the middle of Times Square with what felt like ten million people staring at her, Joe wanted Georgia to play on a street corner with Madison Square Garden behind her, and then strolling through Grand Central Station.

When at last they emerged from the train station, darkness had fallen. Joe turned to Georgia, who felt as if she could fall asleep right there on the sidewalk in the middle of Manhattan, and said, "Georgia, you were wonderful. We'll get you a copy of the video as soon as it's finished."

Georgia said good-bye to Mr. Elden then, and she and her mother and Nana Dana rode back uptown in a cab, Georgia half-asleep. But she woke up fully when her mother put her arm around her shoulder and whispered, "Honey, you were amazing. I'm proud of you."

Nana Dana added, "You really have to come to the city more often. Both of you."

# Chapter 8

# Dana Burley Goldberg

Dana Goldberg had three grandchildren, but she still couldn't get used to being a nana. Or to being called Nana Dana. Her only child, her daughter Francie, had called her Dana, never Mom, yet somehow Dana was now Nana. She didn't feel like a grandmother. She had turned fifty-seven on her last birthday, an age that, when she was six, had seemed positively ancient. But now, well, Dana had one friend her age whose son had just graduated from high school. He was only eighteen. So fifty-seven wasn't terribly old, was it?

Dana looked around the small art studio at the back of her apartment. It was nowhere near the size of the studio she used to have when she and Matthew and Francie had lived in the house on Vandeventer Avenue in Princeton. But she no longer needed so much space. She illustrated fewer books and took on less work these days (her choice). She was tired of deadlines and of getting up at 5:00 a.m. Not that she couldn't handle those things. She just chose not to.

"I'm also not going to work on Sundays anymore," she said aloud. She closed the door to the studio, walked down the hall to the kitchen, made a cup of coffee, and carried it to the living room. She sat in the armchair, the somewhat raggedy one that had made its way from Vandeventer to the smaller house in Princeton after her divorce from Matthew, and finally to this apartment in New York, where Dana hoped to live until she died. After a childhood spent moving around with her restless mother, Dana did not intend to move ever again.

She was reaching for the Sunday *New York Times* and considering cranking up the air conditioner when her phone rang. Dana reached for it and checked the caller ID. Maine, her daughter Francie's number.

"Hi, honey!" Dana said brightly, a greeting that would be appropriate for any member of the Noble family.

"Nana Dana! Guess what!" It was Georgia's excited voice.

"What?"

"I just the saw the video! The one we shot in New York. Mr. Elden — remember him? — emailed me a copy. He said I'll have actual DVDs soon, so I'll send you one. You can see it on your DVD player, since I know you don't really understand your computer. I mean, not that you're . . . It's just that you're sort of old-fashioned. . . . I mean . . ."

Dana laughed. "That's okay. I *am* old-fashioned. You know me and email. I can't wait to have the DVD."

"Nana Dana, this is so exciting! I look professional. Although . . . I'm not the only kid in the video. I guess they filmed other kids some other time and then put the whole thing together. But anyway, it's really cool."

"Honey, that's wonderful. You're a star."

"Yeah. Well, a star who's grounded."

"What?"

"Mom grounded me yesterday. It was so unfair!"

"Tell me what happened."

Georgia sighed loudly. "I didn't *do any*thing."

"But what happened?"

Another sigh. "You know my friends Talia and Ava?"

"Yes."

"Well, their mother said they could ride their bikes to Barnegat Point by themselves. No adult. They asked me to go with them, but Mom said no, and I said Talia and Ava had permission, and Mom said, 'Talia and Ava aren't my daughters,' and I said, 'I'm three months older than Talia and five months older than Ava,' and Mom said something about everyone jumping off a cliff, and then I went to my room and slammed the door and Mom grounded me. Even though Richard is just one year older than me and *he's* allowed to ride to Barnegat Point without an adult."

Dana closed her eyes briefly. At last she said, "I'm sorry, honey. It's no fun being grounded during summer vacation. At least you have your guitar."

"Yeah. You want to hear the song I'm writing? It starts, 'Why did you give birth to me / just to torture me?' Only I don't know what rhymes with 'torture me' so I'm a little stuck." Georgia paused. "Did you know there's no word that rhymes with *orange*?"

Dana settled back into the armchair, smiling. Mothers and daughters were the same in every generation, she supposed. The mothers were unfair and the daughters rebelled. Dana had rebelled against her own mother, and slowly she and Abby had grown apart. Even after Dana had grown up, even after she had become a mother and then a grandmother, she and Abby had maintained a wary distance.

*I should call her,* Dana thought, as she listened to Georgia. *I should call my mother and apologize.*

The list of things for which she should apologize was long. Very long. Going all the way back to the night on the Staten Island Ferry when Dana's father, after an evening involving way too much drinking, had tried to capture his hat as the wind plucked it from his head and sent it sailing out over the bay. He had lunged for it, and Dana had lunged for him. But her father hadn't been able to rescue his hat, and Dana hadn't been able to rescue her father.

She hadn't blamed him, though. Instead she had blamed her mother, who had been throwing up in the ferry's restroom. If her mother had been sober, she would have been at Dana's side and surely the two of them could have pulled her father back. That was what Dana had thought on that unforgettable night, and for weeks afterward. Her mother, who had nagged her husband endlessly about his drinking, had been drunk herself the one time he most needed her.

Then Abby had revealed to Dana and her brother and sister that she was pregnant. Another baby was on the way.

Pregnant.

Abby hadn't been drunk the night of the accident. She'd been ill, with round-the-clock morning sickness.

*And I blamed her,* Dana thought. *For weeks I blamed her for something unthinkable.*

She should have asked her mother why she was sick, but instead she had silently assumed the worst.

"Can you believe it?" Georgia was saying now. "Can you believe she did that? She never listens to me."

What Dana believed was that there were two sides to every story, but what she said was, "Have you tried talking to your mother?"

This was followed by a moment of silence. "What?" Georgia asked finally.

"Have you tried talking to her?"

"No! It's pointless!"

"Maybe your mother has a reason for not wanting you to —"

"The reason is that she's unfair."

It was Dana's turn to sigh.

Georgia continued talking and Dana found herself recalling the freezing, cramped apartment Abby had moved her children into after Nell, the unexpected baby, had been born. It had been one-sixth the size of their old apartment. Dana's wealthy father, whom she had loved more than anyone in the world except possibly her brother, Peter, had left no money when he'd died, no cushion to support his family. Yet somehow, Dana had found a way to blame her mother for everything that had happened after the night on the ferry, starting with the move away from their neighborhood.

The new apartment was like nothing Dana had seen before. Five people living in three tiny rooms. She and her twin sister shared one room, barely big enough to accommodate their beds. Peter's bed and Nell's crib were crammed into the other room, and Abby slept on the couch in the remaining room, which also served as living room and kitchen, and was only minimally bigger than either of the bedrooms. Dana remembered peering in at her mother early one morning, seeing her sound asleep, her arm flung over her face to shield it from the sunlight streaming through the window.

*Get a shade, get curtains, get something,* Dana remembered thinking, even though she had recently seen her mother counting change from the bottom of her purse, hoping she would have enough money for bus fare so she could ride to her shift at the hospital, instead of walking thirty blocks.

Then came the move to Maine. When it had become clear that raising four children in Manhattan by herself on the teensy salary of a desk clerk wasn't going to work, Abby plucked her children out of the city they loved and moved them to the beach cottage in Lewisport, giving away their beloved cat in the process. Dana tried to picture herself in Abby's shoes. Would she have had the courage to do what her mother had done? To hold her family together, to raise her children on her own, to make it all work — somehow — without asking for any help? She didn't know.

They had moved from town to town, from apartment to apartment, and started at one new school after another until one day Dana couldn't take it any longer. She had looked up and down the bleak streets of whatever town they were currently living in, and thought so longingly of Manhattan — and of the shadow of her father that remained there — that she knew she couldn't stay in Maine. Outside her bedroom window in New York had been people and activity and cabs and noise. Outside her current bedroom window was a vaguely sandy street with white houses that looked exactly like one another. That was about it. She had written to her aunt Adele in New York and asked if she could live with her.

The day before Dana had taken the train home — New York had always felt like home, Maine never had — she'd tried once again to explain things to her mother, knowing even as she did so, that she was leaving out the most important thing.

"I have to leave," she had said to Abby.

"I know you do."

"I miss New York too much."

"I know."

What Dana didn't dare say was that New York was where she could feel her father. The pulse of the city was like her father's heartbeat. But how to explain that to her mother? How to say that she chose the memory of her father over her entire living family?

"Nana Dana? Are you there?"

"Sorry, honey. Yes, I'm here. I'm just wool-gathering. That's what your great-grandmother would say."

"Well, do you?"

"Do I what?"

"Think I should make a list? That's what Aunt Kaycee told me once. She said making a list would help me organize my thoughts."

"Yes, make a list," Dana replied, even though she had completely lost track of the conversation and wasn't sure what the list was for.

"Okay. Thanks. I'll let you know what happens. I'll have plenty of time, since I'm *grounded*. And I'll send you the DVD as soon as I can."

"Thank you. I'll talk to you soon."

"Bye. Love you."

"Love you, too."

Dana pressed the Off button, but continued to hold the phone in her hand. It was time to call her mother, to give her the apology she knew she owed her. But where would she start? With the night on the ferry? And what on earth would she say? "Hi, Mom. It's me, Dana. You know the night Dad died? Well, I thought it was your fault. I thought you were drunk, which wasn't true, and that if you'd been sober, you could have saved him, which probably wasn't true either."

She couldn't imagine herself saying this.

Okay, then apologize for not appreciating what her mother went through to hold their family together. "Hi, Mom. It's me, Dana. You know the hardest thing you ever did? Well, I was a teenager at the time and a little wrapped up in myself so all I could see was the road back to New York. Sorry."

She couldn't do it. These were not the right words. And maybe this wasn't the right time.

Dana set the phone back in its cradle.

# Chapter 9

Georgia stood at the front door of the cottage and looked outside at the dreary, dreary morning. She thought of *The Cat in the Hat*, and of Sally and her brother stuck inside their house on the cold, wet day. Across Blue Harbor Lane the waves pounded the rocky shore, sending up showers of spray that were the exact dull gray color of the sky, the ocean, the world.

It was Day 7 of spring vacation, and Day 3 of rain. Boredom had set in. Everyone (everyone except Georgia and her family, it seemed) had gone away for spring break, which is what you were *supposed* to do, wasn't it?

"Why can't *we* go somewhere?" Richard had asked the previous weekend. "Alex is in Boston, and Austin's leaving for *Jamaica* tomorrow."

Henry set his fork down tragically. "Dennis is going to Disney World."

Their father smiled at them. "Well, we simply can't afford a trip, that's all."

"Couldn't we at least go to New York?" Georgia had asked. "We could stay with Nana Dana, or Aunt Kaycee and Uncle Mitch. That wouldn't cost anything."

"The train fare would cost something," Mr. Noble had replied.

"But there won't be anyone around this week," said Richard with a distinct whine.

"No one," added Henry. "Not a single person. The whole week."

"What are we supposed to do with ourselves?" asked Georgia.

"For heaven's sake, you have a week off from school," said their mother. "That should count for something."

This was met with silence.

"Maybe we could have a few treats," Mr. Noble said finally. "We'll go to the movies tomorrow. And one night we'll go out for ice cream."

The next few days had been more fun than Georgia had predicted. Talia, Penny, and Ava were away, but Georgia found that she liked going into town by herself. She stopped in at the stores and talked to the shopkeepers. One day her mother dropped her off at the Barnegat Point library and she spent four delicious hours there, curled up on a beanbag chair in the children's room with a stack of books. Another day she and Richard and Henry made kites and sailed them in their yard, watching as they jerked and fluttered their way across the road and out over the ocean.

Then the rain had arrived.

On Day 1 Georgia and her brothers had held a Monopoly tournament.

On Day 2 their mother, desperate to continue working on her current novel, had moved her computer into the kitchen and relaxed her television rule, allowing Georgia, Richard, and Henry to watch an *I Love Lucy* marathon — hours and hours of the adventures of Lucy, Ricky, Ethel, and Fred.

Now it was Friday and the rain was still falling. Georgia stood dully at the front door, arms crossed. She couldn't think of a single thing she wanted to do, and had rejected every suggestion her mother had made over breakfast that morning: write a new song, go back to the library, put on a play with her brothers, help her father at the store.

Behind her she heard Henry say, "Let's dress up Noelle."

"That's a *girl* suggestion," was Richard's derisive reply.

"I'm not a girl!"

"Well, you sound like one. Like a little baby girl."

"I'm *seven!*"

"Kids!" their mother called.

Georgia realized that the clacking of the computer had stopped. She turned to her brothers. "Good one," she said. "Now Mom's mad."

But instead Mrs. Noble said, "Lunchtime. Come help me make sandwiches."

"I don't want a sandwich," said Richard.

"I'm not hungry," said Henry.

"Do we have to?" asked Georgia.

"You're driving me crazy," their mother replied. "Just come in here and be positive."

"B positive is a blood type," said Georgia, and she rolled her eyes.

Richard smirked.

Mrs. Noble stepped into the living room. "All right," she said in a low voice that Georgia recognized with alarm. "I have had about enough. Come into the kitchen this very minute, all three of you, and don't say a single word. Not one. You're acting like spoiled brats. I'm very sorry your friends went away and you had to stay here, but you have a roof over your heads and a refrigerator full of food, which is more than lots of children have. So march yourselves in here — not a word — make your sandwiches, eat them, and then go think about your lives."

A sullen, silent lunch followed. As soon as the plates had been cleared, Mrs. Noble set her computer on the table, sat down, and with her back turned, said, "Go. Leave me in peace. If I hear so much as one cross word, believe me, I'll think up a very creative punishment."

Georgia retreated to her room. She sat on her bed and looked into the backyard. She could hear the *clackety-clack* of her mother at work. She was reaching for her guitar when out of nowhere, Richard appeared, grabbed the guitar, held it above his head, and cried, "I'm a rock star, baby! I am so cool! Notice me! Notice me!" He strummed the strings vigorously.

"Richard, give it!" cried Georgia. She bounded off the bed and jumped to save her prize possession from her twelve-year-old brother. "You aren't playing it right. You're going to break the strings."

Richard leaped out of the way.

"Give! It!" Georgia tackled him and he lost his balance, falling on his hands and knees, the guitar dropping onto the bed.

"Hey!" exclaimed Richard. "What do you think you're —"

"Never touch that again!" Georgia straddled Richard, bouncing on his shoulders, but he flipped her to the floor as easily as if she were a pancake.

Georgia saw her winter boots beside the dresser and reached for one. Richard was quicker. He snatched it, jumped to his feet, held it above his head, and let it fly. Georgia ducked and the boot hit the wall by her bed, hard.

Once again the clacking stopped. Georgia stared at her brother.

*A very creative punishment.*

In a flash, Richard was out of her room. Georgia hastily closed the door behind him. Then she turned to look at her wall. The wood paneling, lovingly put up almost a hundred years earlier by her great-great-grandfather, was nearly indestructible, but Georgia didn't want to see so much as a scuff mark, considering the mood her mother was in.

What she saw was worse, way worse. A portion of the wall had come away and dropped to the floor. Georgia gasped, and automatically looked toward her door, wishing she could lock it. She paused, listening for sounds from the living room, but heard only Henry's voice: "I didn't do anything!"

She bent over to pick up the paneling, praying that she could jam it back in place, but as she held it in her hands she noticed that it was in the shape of a perfect rectangle. No jagged edges, not so much as a splintered fragment.

Well, that was weird. How could the boards break apart like that? She got to her feet and examined the wall. To her surprise, she found a rectangular hole by her bed. An actual hole, a space behind the wall. A secret panel, just like in a detective story.

Georgia laid the section of wall on her dresser and reached for her flashlight. She shined it down into the compartment . . . and gasped. Gingerly, since surely there were spiders — or worse — in the dark space, she reached inside. Her fingers closed over a book. She pulled it out.

Not a book, she realized. A journal. A very dusty old journal.

Georgia blew the dust from the cover, then wiped it with a Kleenex. The cover was leather, black and peeling. In cracked gold letters were the simple words: MY DIARY. Carefully she opened the book. It was bound with three brass rings, and the pages were filled with line after line of spidery blue handwriting.

Whose?

Georgia flipped to the front of the journal. Written on the inside cover was the name *Eleanor Durbin Nichols*.

Eleanor, Georgia thought. Eleanor Nichols. Nell Nichols? Was this the Eleanor Nichols who was Great-Grandma Abby's mother? The Eleanor from whom Georgia had gotten one of her middle names? Georgia remembered something her great-grandmother had told her after the Nobles had moved to the cottage. "When I was a little girl," she had said, "my sister Rose and I slept upstairs where your parents sleep now. Your room belonged to my parents, Georgia. To Nell and Luther."

*This diary was my great-great-grandmother's,* Georgia thought, and she felt a little breathless. She flipped to a page in the middle of the book and stared at the faded ink. The handwriting was hard to decipher.

"'. . . sunny day,'" Georgia read aloud, starting at the top of the left-hand page. She squinted. "'Abby and Rose took Adele all morning. So hard to get out of bed. I'm a terrible example. Abby is more a mother than I.'"

Georgia frowned. She flipped to the next page, looking for a date. June 5th, 1938. How old would Nell Nichols have been then? It seemed to Georgia that Great-Grandma Abby's mother had died young. She thought for a moment and recalled a conversation with Great-Grandma from . . . how long ago? Three years? Four? She'd been sitting in

Great-Grandma's lap at a picnic, leaning against her chest and idly asking questions. *How old were you when you moved to the big house in town? Have you ever seen a snake? When did your mother die?* The answers to these questions were: *About eleven; Once;* and *When I was a teenager. Mama had always been frail, and then one summer she got sick, and grew weaker and weaker, and finally died in her sleep.*

Georgia turned pages rapidly and discovered that the journal entries ended abruptly just a few weeks later, at the end of July, and were followed by many blank pages.

Georgia set the journal on her bed and shined the flashlight into the hole again, pausing briefly to listen for sounds from the living room. Nothing. In the weak light she could see more hidden books. She pulled them out one by one. There were four, in different sizes with different covers: a small red one that fastened with a brass clasp; two larger black journals, one of which was tied with a white ribbon; and a dark blue one with the spine dangling, its clasp broken. They all belonged to Nell, although in the front of the blue one her name appeared as *Eleanor Richmond Durbin.*

Georgia looked at the dates each journal covered, and arranged the books in chronological order. The blue one was the oldest. It began at the end of 1917. The two black ones covered the 1920s, and the small red one began in 1930. The one Georgia had discovered first was actually the last. Had it ended with Nell's death?

Georgia returned the four older journals to their hiding place and leaned the panel against the wall. Then she settled on her bed with the final journal. She discovered that there were many gaps in time, because Nell hadn't written in the journal every day. Sometimes she wrote every few days, then skipped several months. At one point a year went by.

Georgia stopped at an entry dated February 14th, 1938.

*Adele's birthday today. Three years old. So many presents, and her favorite is a sucker, funny girl. She asked if Fred could come to her party. I can't explain, can't explain.*

*Who's Fred?* Georgia wondered. She flipped backward and read about a little boy — the only boy in the family. Great-Grandma Abby's brother. Born "wrong" and — was he sent away? It seemed so. Sent away by Nell's husband, Luther, without her permission or even her knowledge.

*My heart hurts,* Nell wrote. *My heart is broken.*

Georgia skipped ahead again. The entries became even bleaker. She found herself reading about a woman in pain. Not physical pain, she realized, but emotional pain.

*Anguish,* Nell wrote. *It's anguish. How can I explain how much this hurts? "Carry on!" says Ellen. So brightly. I can't simply carry on. It isn't that easy.*

*I'm a burden.*

Another entry: *What kind of mother am I? Some days I don't want to see my children.*

*My heart hurts,* she wrote over and over again.

Georgia's own heart began to flip-flop. She felt that she was beginning to know a horrible truth, one that Great-Grandma Abby probably didn't know. One that perhaps no one knew.

On the final pages Nell wrote: *It just hurts so much. I'm a coward. So much pain. I can't stop crying. This is too hard, too hard. I can't do it anymore.*

In that instant Georgia knew exactly what *do it* meant. It meant *live.* Nell couldn't live any longer. What had happened? She had ended her life, Georgia was certain of that. She had ended it shortly after her last journal entry.

Georgia longed to share the journals with her great-grandmother. But she couldn't, could she? All these years, these decades, her great-grandmother had lived without the horrible truth that Georgia had discovered. And perhaps that was as it should be.

Georgia opened her door silently and peeked into the living room. Richard and Henry were lying feet-to-feet on the couch, reading comic books. Noelle dozed on the floor beneath them. The clacking of the computer had resumed.

Georgia closed her door again and slipped the final journal back into the hidey-hole. She pressed the panel into place. Then she lay on her bed and cried.

# Chapter 10

The trouble with going to school in Barnegat Point was that, well, it was in Barnegat Point, not in Lewisport, which meant that the Lewisport students had to be driven there and back every day. In the Nobles' case, someone had to drive Georgia and Richard to the middle school and Henry to the elementary school. When the weather was nice, Mrs. Noble occasionally allowed Richard, and now Georgia, to ride their bikes into Barnegat Point, but this didn't happen often, and anyway, the ride was long.

Today, a slushy, frigid January afternoon, Georgia stood in front of the middle school with Ava and Talia, burdened by their backpacks, blowing on her mittened hands, and stepping from one foot to the other.

"Where's your mom?" Talia asked Ava.

"She'll be here." Ava looked at her watch. "Hey, where's Richard? Isn't he coming with us?"

"He's supposed to," said Georgia. "But you know Richard."

Richard's behavior recently had been unpredictable. He'd turned thirteen the week before, not that that had anything to do with anything. When he'd begun seventh grade in the fall, he'd also begun keeping his own hours, ignoring the rules his parents set for him. A 9:00 curfew meant nothing. Richard couldn't drive yet, of course, but he had friends who could, and he came home whenever he felt like it: at 11:00 on a school night, later on weekend nights. When his enraged parents asked him what he thought he was doing, he replied, "Hanging out." Sometimes he didn't reply at all, just walked past the Nobles and into the bedroom he shared with Henry. If a punishment was meted out, Richard ignored it.

"What's my mom supposed to do if Richard isn't here when she comes?" asked Ava.

Georgia shrugged. "Just leave. He won't care. He'll find someone else to drive him home."

Georgia's mind was on other things. One was the empty storefront in Lewisport. It was the building that had housed the dollhouse store, and after that had finally (*finally*) failed, her father's juice bar. The juice bar had been as unsuccessful as the store — but mercifully had lasted only several months. Now it too had closed, and the building stood empty.

Mr. Noble had done a lot of the carpooling recently.

"He doesn't have anything else to do with his life," Richard had muttered to Georgia one afternoon.

Georgia had rounded on him. "Yes, he does!" she'd said loudly, then lowered her voice, realizing her father was just steps away in the kitchen. "Yes, he does," she'd whispered.

"Name one thing," Richard demanded.

Georgia's face had reddened. "He's thinking about a new business."

Richard snorted. "Good luck with that."

"Well, if you know all the answers, what do *you* think he should do?"

"Teach. He's a teacher. That's what he's supposed to do."

"Where? There aren't any teaching jobs around here."

"Well, he could do something," said Richard, but suddenly he looked and sounded defeated.

This was not unusual for Richard, as he brought home one failed test, one pathetic report card, after another.

"You're in danger of being asked to repeat seventh grade," his mother had warned him recently.

"So?"

"Do you *want* to stay back?"

"I don't care."

"If you would just settle down and pay attention to your

assignments you could do very well," said his father. "I'd be happy to tutor you."

"I don't care about school!"

Georgia had retreated to her room then. She'd closed the door quietly and pulled out her guitar.

Now she squinted into the foggy afternoon light. "There's your mom," she said to Ava, as a blue Subaru pulled into the school parking lot.

The girls piled into the car.

"Where's Richard?" asked Ava's mother.

"He's not coming," Georgia replied. She saw Mrs. Norwood glance at her in the rearview mirror and she lowered her eyes.

"All right then. Off we go."

Fifteen minutes later, Mrs. Norwood pulled up in front of the cottage.

"Bye!" called Talia and Ava.

Georgia wriggled out of the car. "Bye," she replied. "Thank you, Mrs. Norwood."

Georgia stood for a moment looking at the little house. Her father's car was in the driveway, which was not unusual. The lights were on both downstairs and upstairs, which *was* unusual. Georgia entered the house, stepping over Noelle, and hanging her wet coat on the peg by the door.

"Hello?" she called.

Henry peered out of his room. "Don't go upstairs," he whispered.

"What? Why not?"

"Something's going on. Mom and Dad are both up there, and Mom said not to go up."

Georgia frowned. "Well, I'm going up anyway."

"No, don't," said Henry, reaching for her. "I think Dad's crying."

Georgia twisted away from him and ran to her parents' room. She heard soft footsteps behind her and saw Henry hesitate at the bottom of the staircase. "Stay there," she told him. Then she called out, "Mom? Dad?" When there wasn't any answer, she knocked on their door.

"Not now," her father called back.

"What's wrong?"

"I said, not now."

"Please let me come in."

Georgia heard whispered voices, and a moment later her mother opened the door. Georgia leaned around her. A suitcase was on the bed. It was half-packed, with more clothes tossed on the bed and others spilling from hangers in the closet.

"What's going on?" Georgia asked.

Her mother turned to her father. "Why don't you tell her?" There was an edge to her voice.

"Tell me what?" Georgia bit her lip. She took a step into the room.

Her father, who had been busily arranging things in the suitcase, sat on the bed and faced her. Georgia could see that Henry had been right. Her father was crying.

"Tell me what?" she said again.

Her father patted the bed. "Come sit next to me, Georgie Girl."

Georgia sat. She looked at her hands and realized they were shaking.

"Honey," said her father, and he reached for her hands, holding them tightly in his until the trembling stopped. "I've decided . . . I've decided to go away for a while."

"Go away? What, like on a trip?" Then something occurred to her. "Are you going to look for work?" She didn't want to move away from Lewisport, but if her father found a job somewhere else, moving might not be the worst thing in the world.

Her father sighed. Across the room, her mother shook her head in disgust.

"No," he said. "I just need a little time to figure some things out."

Georgia frowned. "Figure what things out? Why can't you do that here?"

"I need to figure out what to do with myself, with my life. The store failed. The juice bar failed. I can't find a job. *I* feel like a failure. I think I need a little space for thinking. I need to be somewhere different."

Georgia's mother sank into the armchair by the window and put her face in her hands.

"Mom?" said Georgia.

"I'm okay. It's going to be okay."

Georgia turned back to her father. "Where are you going? How long will you be gone?"

"I'm going to stay with Aunt Kaycee and Uncle Mitch —"

"Aunt Kaycee and Uncle Mitch? Why are you going all the way to New York?"

"Georgia, I don't have the answers right now. I'm sorry. I just need to get away."

"From us?" Georgia let go of her father's hands and stood up. "You need to get away from us? That's what you mean, isn't it?"

"No, not from you," said her father. "It's hard to explain. I need to think."

"But why can't you think here? With your family?" Georgia looked at her mother, who shrugged.

"I'm sorry, honey," her father answered. "This doesn't have anything to do with you."

"Yes, it does! You're leaving me." Georgia felt tears spring to her eyes.

"I'm leaving, but I'm not leaving you. Or your mother or your brothers. I'm leaving in order to make things better. I need to figure out what to do. I need some answers."

Georgia stood in the doorway. "Okay," she said at last. "I don't understand, but okay." She wiped her eyes and walked down the stairs and into her room, where she found Noelle curled on her bed. Henry knocked on her door. "Go away," said Georgia. "I'll talk to you later."

She heard his footsteps pad slowly back toward his room.

Twenty minutes later Georgia heard more footsteps. Her parents were coming downstairs. She opened her door and saw her father lugging his suitcase into the living room. Her mother walked heavily behind him and into the kitchen, where Georgia heard the refrigerator open.

"Henry?" said their father. "Could I talk to you for a minute?"

Henry, eyes puffy and red, emerged from his bedroom.

Georgia once again closed herself into her room. She couldn't bear to hear what their father would say to Henry, but her closed door didn't muffle Henry's sobs.

At last, with a sigh, she joined her father and Henry in the living room.

"When . . . are . . . you . . . coming . . . back?" Henry was asking, the words leaving his mouth in gasps.

"I don't know, but as soon as I can."

The front door opened and Richard strode in. "Hey," he said, looking from Georgia to his father to Henry. "What's wrong?"

"Sit down," said their father.

Richard listened for about twenty seconds before he slammed his backpack onto the floor and shouted, "This is crap! This is *crap!*" He stormed into his room and slammed the door.

"That went well," said their mother from the kitchen.

Georgia watched their father. He set his suitcase by the front door and put on his winter coat. Then he kissed Georgia and Henry. He knocked lightly on Richard's door and called, "I'll be back soon."

"You are such a liar," was Richard's reply.

Georgia's mother busied herself in the kitchen.

"Good-bye," Mr. Noble said to her, standing uncertainly in the doorway.

The refrigerator door closed. A cabinet door opened.

Georgia's father picked up his suitcase, carried it outside, got into his car, and backed it onto Blue Harbor Lane.

Georgia watched the taillights disappear around the bend. Then she crept into the kitchen and hugged her mother from behind. "I'll help you make supper," she said.

Supper was eaten in silence.

When it was over, Georgia cleaned up the kitchen. She refused to cry. She helped Henry with a math work sheet, then did her own homework. Richard switched the television on and the four Nobles gathered in front of it, silently and humorlessly watching reruns of *Seinfeld*.

"Bedtime," said their mother eventually, long after Henry's usual school night bedtime.

Richard and Henry slogged into their room.

Georgia turned to her mother. "Do you think he's coming back?" she whispered.

Her mother shook her head. "I don't know."

# Chapter 11

Georgia sat on an iron bench in her small backyard and looked up at the cloudless blue sky. She closed her eyes and listened to the sound of the surf across Blue Harbor Lane, breathed in the scents of salt and sand and the lavender plants at her feet. She remembered Great-Grandma Abby once telling her about two rosebushes that used to grow not far from where she was sitting. Georgia opened her eyes, left the bench, and scuffed around the yard. No sign of where the rosebushes had once grown but, she realized, Great-Grandma must have been talking about a time seventy-five years or more in the past.

The rosebushes had been special to Great-Grandma's mother, Nell. The blooms on the bushes had been a lovely deep pink, Great-Grandma had said, but that wasn't why the bushes had been special. They'd been special because of what they'd represented.

"What did they represent?" Georgia had wanted to know.

Great-Grandma Abby had stared off into space before she spoke. "My father planted a bush for each of the babies my mother gave birth to that didn't live, that never even drew a breath of life. One for a little girl named Millicent and one for a little boy named Luther, after my father. First I was born, then my sister Rose was born, and then came Millicent and Luther. My mother never got over them. No mother expects to see her children die before she does. It isn't the natural order of things."

Georgia had found that a supremely unsatisfying explanation. She looked again for the spots where two sad rosebushes might once have grown, but found nothing. She knew they had eventually been moved to the garden of the big house in Barnegat Point when Great-Grandma Abby's father had become wealthy and they had left the little beach cottage behind. The cottage had become a vacation house then, and now it was once again a home. Georgia wished it were a home with two old rosebushes by the iron bench.

"Georgia?" her father called from the back door. "What are you doing out there? Want to go into town with me?"

The idea of walking to Lewisport's collection of stores and businesses was appealing, but Georgia was enjoying this quiet, lazy morning in the middle of a three-day weekend. As usual, her friends had gone away for the vacation. Ava and the Norwoods were spending Memorial Day with relatives in Portland, and Penny and Talia and their parents had flown to Chicago for a wedding. The Nobles, on the other hand, were having another vacation at home.

No amount of begging by Richard and Henry had been able to change their parents' minds. (Georgia had not bothered to beg.)

"We can't afford to go anywhere and that's that," Mr. Noble had said the first time the subject arose.

Since her father was still without a job, this had made perfect sense to Georgia. She was just glad he was home again. He had spent several weeks with his sister, Kaycee, and her husband when he'd needed to figure things out. Then he'd returned to Lewisport and announced that he knew what to do with his life after all. He was going to sell real estate. And he did. He'd sold a fishing shack on an inlet not far from Blue Harbor Lane. He'd sold two small homes that were miles from the beach and couldn't be considered vacation property. He'd sold a slightly larger house that had been lived in by a couple for close to sixty years and badly needed a new septic system in addition to all new appliances and a complete makeover.

"This isn't working," Georgia's father finally said in disgust. Eight months after he returned from Kaycee's, he left again. But two weeks later his car pulled into the driveway and he'd announced once more that he was home.

"Now what?" asked Mrs. Noble, shaking her head.

"I don't know. Back to real estate, I suppose."

"Back to real estate?" exclaimed Richard when he heard the news. It was late, eleven thirty on a school night, and Richard had just walked through the door. No one mentioned the fact that he had missed his curfew. "Don't you sometimes wonder why we left Princeton?" he asked.

"Every day," his father had replied, rubbing his eyes. "Every single day."

Now Georgia blinked in the sunlight, having almost forgotten what her father had asked her. "Go into town?" she repeated. "I guess not. But thanks. I'm going to practice for a while." She patted her guitar, which was sitting beside her on the bench. "Maybe Henry will go with you."

Five minutes later Georgia watched her father and Henry stride down Blue Harbor, identical baseball caps worn backward on their heads. She picked up her guitar and strummed it thoughtfully. Her lessons with Mr. Elden were going well. She took only private lessons now that she was in middle school. When she'd graduated from the elementary school, she'd entertained the hope that Mr. Elden would move on to the middle school with her, but of course that hadn't happened. He was a beloved fixture at BP Elementary. Georgia felt lucky that her parents always found a way to pay for her private lessons.

Now if she could just put together a band of her own. That was her dream: to play guitar in a band. But Penny and Talia, who took flute lessons, were hopeless and unenthusiastic musicians, and Ava, who had played keyboard in the elementary school band, had given that up, saying that her dog could play better than she could. (Privately, Georgia agreed with her.)

So Georgia sat on the bench and strummed and daydreamed and imagined outfits that she would one day wear onstage.

"Honey?" her mother called to her from the kitchen window. "Are you wearing sunblock?"

"No." Georgia set down her guitar. "I was about to come inside, though."

"What are you going to do today?"

"I don't know. Nothing. Which is fine with me."

The seventh graders had been burdened with homework lately, in addition to studying for final exams. Georgia was happy for a little island of freedom and free time.

She entered the cottage, which was cool and dim and smelled of fresh air and the warm days of spring, sat on her bed, and carefully put her guitar back in its case. She thought about the rosebushes again. She didn't know why they kept creeping back into her thoughts.

Georgia's mind flew to the journals she'd found two years earlier. She remembered skimming through the last one and discovering Nell's awful secret — and then hastily closing them into their hiding place. She hadn't looked at them since.

"The rosebushes," Georgia said aloud. "Maybe I can read what Nell wrote about the babies."

She crossed her room and quietly closed her door. Then she examined the panel on the wall. She realized she didn't know how to open it. When Richard had thrown her boot at it two years ago, it had seemed to pop open on its own.

Georgia pressed the center of the panel lightly. Nothing happened.

She ran her fingers along the edges of the panel. Nothing.

She pressed the left side of the panel — and the right side sprang away from the wall. Georgia gripped the panel before it could fall to the floor. She placed it on her bed. Then she reached her hand into the dark space, but withdrew it quickly and reached for her flashlight as an image of her hand closing over a spider came to mind.

Georgia shined the light into the hole. There they were, in an untidy stack. Five ancient journals. She pulled out the top one, recalling that it was Nell's last. Below it were the four earlier ones. Georgia set all five on her bed and once again arranged them chronologically. She wanted to read about the babies, the lost babies, but remembering what she had learned about the end of Nell's life, she realized now that she wanted to start at the beginning and read the journals in order. She wanted to understand Nell. Georgia reached for the blue journal with the dangling spine and the broken clasp.

That was how Georgia Eleanor Goldberg Noble entered the life of her great-great-grandmother Eleanor Richmond Durbin at the end of 1917.

Georgia considered the date. Late 1917. Close to the end of the first world war. Although, she realized, back then it wouldn't have been called World War One, because nobody knew there would be another world war. It was just the World War, she supposed. The war to end all wars.

In 1917 Eleanor Durbin was, as far as Georgia could tell, about eighteen years old. Georgia didn't know when her great-great-grandmother had been born, but at the start of the journal, Nell was working in a milliner's shop (it took Georgia some time to figure out that a milliner's shop sold hats), and she had apparently graduated from high school recently.

Eighteen years old, already working, living with her parents, and no mention of going off to college. Nell was an adult, not quite independent yet, but she had moved into the next phase of her life. Georgia couldn't imagine being in Nell's situation in just five years.

The village where Nell lived with her parents was called St. George. Nell's older sister, Betty, lived there, too, with her new husband, Marshall. Georgia had heard of St. George. It wasn't far away, although it wasn't any village now. It was a bustling town.

Not in 1917, though.

In 1917 the St. George described by Nell Durbin was even smaller than Lewisport was now, but it did have a few stores, and Georgia's great-great-grandmother had worked in the hat shop. She had made hats and she had sold hats. And in the quiet moments between, she had dreamed about Ralph Saunders, a boy she had known since they were in third grade.

*Perhaps my Ralph will come by the shop at the end of the day to walk me home,* Nell wrote.

And in another entry: *One day my Ralph and I will have the perfect wedding.*

*My Ralph,* thought Georgia. How nice to have a boy you could call your own.

Nell wrote often about marrying Ralph. She recalled that they were in fourth grade the first time he proposed to her.

*We held a wedding on the beach!* she wrote giddily. *I wore my best church dress and Ralph wore his best suit. We were barefoot. Betty, who was eleven, was the minister. Edward* (Ralph's brother, Georgia realized) *was the ring bearer. Four of our classmates came to watch.*

Apparently the ceremony had been slightly marred by two other boys from their class who had hidden behind some rocks on the beach and leaped out shrieking just as Ralph was about to slip a ring on Nell's finger.

*A ring of twined dandelion stems,* Nell wrote. *I thought it was the loveliest ring I'd ever seen.*

Nell and Ralph had graduated from grammar school and gone on to high school in Barnegat Point. They'd been sweethearts from the day they entered until the day they graduated. And then Ralph had been called to join the army.

*He was proud. Proud to be called to serve his country, even though the war should be coming to an end soon.*

Before he left, he proposed to Nell again. This time the proposal was serious. *Onto my finger he slipped a ring of silver with a tiny diamond chip in the center. He wanted to know if I would marry him when he came home. Of course I said yes. Of course!*

Nell passed her days working in the hat shop and dreaming of her wedding and the life she and Ralph would have. They would move to Barnegat Point, she thought. A town bigger than St. George would be nice.

*We will live in a little house near the center of town. We'll have three children. A boy, a girl, and another boy. The first boy will be named Ralph. The girl will be named Eleanor. And the second boy, I think, should be named James. Or maybe Jonathan.*

Then one evening not long after Nell had arrived home from the hat shop, a knock had come at the door. The Durbins were eating supper, and Nell's mother was displeased by the interruption.

"I'd better see who it is," said Nell. She folded her napkin and set it by her plate.

Then she opened the front door.

*There are some things a person doesn't ever forget. Images that stay in your mind like a photograph. That scene . . . Edward standing on the porch with his hat in his hands, his head bowed. The image is in black and white and brown.*

Nell felt her knees buckle then, but she remained standing. She embraced Edward after he had given her the news and then she went inside to tell her family that Ralph wouldn't be coming home. His plane had been shot down, and although his body hadn't been found and he was listed as missing in action, he was presumed dead.

Georgia thought that this entry would be followed by pages and pages of grief, by descriptions of a memorial service, perhaps, of tearful conversations with Betty.

Instead there was a long gap. Days went by. Then this abrupt note:

*I have had to let go of the dream of our future together.*

# Chapter 12

*Sunday, May 25th, 2008*

The morning rolled on, the house quiet except for the sounds of Georgia's mother as she tidied the kitchen, made coffee, checked her email, spoke on the phone. Georgia read through the first journal, fascinated. How quickly Nell's plans had come apart, as quickly as if they had been a glass that had shattered. In the weeks that followed, her family had tried to console her, but Nell couldn't let go of her plans for the wedding, the house in Barnegat Point, the babies.

*Ralph could still come back,* she confided in the journal. *He's listed as missing in action. Missing.*

But months had gone by and finally a year had passed since Edward had delivered the terrible news to Nell.

As Georgia read the story of Nell's life she was aware of how much time went by between some entries. A month or more, and then Nell would write in a burst, long entries every single day. On the one-year anniversary of the news of Ralph's disappearance, Nell wrote simply: *A year has passed.*

*An entire year. I walk into town and nothing has changed. The shop is the same, the streets are the same. Home is the same.*

*Still, everything has changed. Ralph's family is gone.*

(Georgia didn't know where they had gone or when they had left. Nell hadn't written about it.)

Then came an entry that caught Georgia's eye. It was dated August 17th, 1919, and in it Georgia found the first reference to Luther Nichols.

"Nell's husband," Georgia murmured. "Great-Grandma Abby's father."

They had met at an ice-cream social. (Georgia had to stop reading the journal, get out her laptop, and find out what an ice-cream social was. It turned out to be a gathering, probably held at a church, the purpose of which mainly seemed to be socializing over ice cream, which seemed like an enormously good idea to Georgia.)

*He told me he's just moved here from Connecticut. He wanted to know my name and brought me ice cream and asked Father if he could call on me sometime. Mother is pleased.*

The courtship seemed to progress rather quickly, Georgia thought. Luther was building a cottage for her in Lewisport. That seemed to mean a lot to Nell. And to her parents.

*He's making the furniture, too. All of it with his own hands. Father is impressed.*

But there was also a hint, if not of trouble exactly, then of a sense that things were not quite right: *He doesn't like Faye. That much is clear.* (Faye, Georgia knew, was Nell's best friend from school.) *He doesn't want to spend time with her, and doesn't want me to see her either. He seems to want me for himself. I try to feel flattered, but the effect is of smothering.*

A mere two months later, Luther asked Nell's father for her hand in marriage. When he agreed, Luther proposed to Nell. She accepted and he gave her a plain silver band.

*Nothing fancy. We must save our money. I don't understand, though. As soon as the ring was on my finger, he said I'm to leave my position at the shop. He said no wife of his will go to work. He doesn't want anyone thinking he can't support his family.*

*Still . . . his family! That means he wants children. Three boys, he says. (What will happen if I give him girls?)*

Georgia read on as Nell's new life unfolded. She and Luther moved not to Barnegat Point, but to the cottage in which Georgia Noble was at that very moment sitting.

Two years after their wedding, Nell gave birth to their first child, Abigail Cora Nichols.

*My great-grandmother,* thought Georgia. *Great-Grandma Abby.*

Nell wrote: *He isn't pleased. This isn't what he wanted. I didn't give him a boy. He holds the baby, but there's no light in his eyes. He doesn't love her yet.*

Georgia felt her stomach drop. What kind of father didn't love his own child?

The first journal ended, and Georgia immediately opened the next one.

Two years later, she read, another girl was born. Rose.

*How I long to share this news with Ralph. No, how I wish Ralph were the father of the girls. He would love them. He would love them no matter what.*

"Lunchtime!" called Mrs. Noble from the kitchen, and Georgia jumped. She realized that her father and Henry had returned, and then she heard Richard's voice, too. Her whole family was at home and she hadn't noticed. She was lost in Nell's world of 1924; her life with a man who, Georgia suspected, she didn't love after all, and with two little girls Luther didn't want.

"Coming!" said Georgia, glad for a break.

But as soon as lunch was over she retreated to her bedroom, settled Noelle in her lap, and picked up the old journal.

After Rose's birth, Nell's entries became even more sparse. There were notes here and there — Abby's first steps; a trip to visit Nell's parents, who had moved away from St. George; Christmas with Betty and Marshall and their children. Mundane entries that continued into the third journal until the summer of 1927 when Georgia came across the name Millicent Pryor Nichols.

"The first baby," she said. "The first baby that died."

*The tears keep falling,* Nell wrote. *They fall and fall and fall. Luther is past being annoyed with me. Now he doesn't know what to do. Some days I can't keep track of Abby and Rose.*

Georgia did some math and realized that Abby and Rose were five and three.

*I told Luther I want some way to mark Millicent's birth. Luther didn't understand. She has to mean something, I explained. He planted a rosebush in the yard. "It's where you can see it," he said. Now he expects me to go on with our life. But I can't stop looking at the rosebush.*

The rosebush wasn't put there out of love, Georgia thought. Luther had planted it so Nell would stop crying and start cleaning the house again. He had planted it for the wrong reason, and it had the wrong effect. Nell couldn't look at it without thinking of her lost little girl.

The second rosebush had been planted the following year, when Luther Randolph Nichols Jr. had been born. A boy. A boy for Luther, but he hadn't lived.

How could Nell and Luther stand it? Georgia wondered. How could any of them stand it?

Then, halfway through the third journal, Georgia read an entry that astounded her. It was dated March 24th, 1929.

*Of all things — I got a letter from Ralph today.*

From *Ralph*? Georgia wondered if Nell had made a mistake, had written the wrong name. In almost the same instant, she suspected that it was no mistake, and she suddenly knew why the journals were hidden in the wall of the cottage. Nell had to keep them from Luther. It was imperative that she keep them from him. He must never see the things she was writing. Georgia realized with a pang of hurt for Nell that it must have become much more difficult for her to pour her feelings onto the pages after her family had finally moved to Barnegat Point and used the beach cottage only as a vacation spot. Unless she had had an equally good hiding spot for the journals after they moved to the new house, she would have had to save her thoughts for visits to the cottage.

*Nell's secret life,* thought Georgia.

She read on. Yes, Nell had received a letter from Ralph Saunders in March of 1929, more than ten years after she had heard the news that he was presumed dead.

It was a long letter, apparently. It must have been, since Nell detailed all that had happened to Ralph in the past decade.

And what did Nell do with that letter? Georgia wondered. She flipped through the last few pages of the journal expecting a fat envelope to drop out. Then she flipped carefully through the other journals. Nothing. She shined the flashlight in the hidey-hole. Nothing but dust. If Nell hadn't hidden the letter then she couldn't have kept it, Georgia realized. She wouldn't have risked Luther finding it.

Georgia envisioned Nell reading the letter, reading it again — and maybe again and again — then tearing it into fine pieces, crossing Blue Harbor Lane, and scattering the bits of paper in the ocean, like ashes.

She turned back to the journal. Nell might not have kept the letter itself, but she had written about its contents, and Georgia read on eagerly.

When Ralph's plane had been shot down he had been injured seriously and had spent nearly two years recovering in a hospital in London. He had no identification and was suffering from something Georgia didn't quite understand from Nell's description, but decided must be some sort of brain trauma. Also, his face had been disfigured in the accident.

Georgia set the journal down. *This was almost like that movie The English Patient*, she thought. *So romantic.* Except maybe not very romantic at all when your fiancée is at home in Maine, first mourning your loss, and then getting on with a life that no longer includes you.

By the time Ralph had recovered enough to explain to the hospital staff who he was — and after he had finally managed to locate his family, who by then were living near relatives in Bar Harbor — he instructed his parents not to contact Nell. He didn't want her to see his ravaged face. Eventually, he learned that she had wed Luther, and he decided to start a new life of his own. But now, with a decade gone, still unmarried and still longing for the girl he once married barefoot on the beach in St. George, he decided to contact her after all. He just wanted to see her.

*And so,* Nell wrote, *we have agreed to meet.*

"What?!" cried Georgia. "They agreed to meet?!" How was that going to happen? What would Nell tell Luther? Surely, timid, obedient Eleanor Durbin Nichols wasn't daring enough to go behind his back.

But that's exactly what she'd done.

Heart pounding, Georgia turned the page.

*He'll be here in ten days!* Nell had written, in a voice much lighter than before. She sounded buoyant, nearly effervescent. *The visit is planned for the day Luther will be in Portland. I must instruct the girls not to say anything about Ralph's face. I need to prepare them, Rose especially. We shall have a picnic. A picnic in the back garden.*

The next entry was dated eleven days later, and Georgia practically tore the page in her eagerness to start reading.

*Heaven,* the entry began. *It was heaven. Heaven having Ralph here. The girls were angels. They sat in his lap and asked for stories. Rose patted his face, but said nothing. Abby smiled at him. Then she asked if he knew the tale of Red Riding Hood, and he said he did. He told it as naturally as a father might* (Here several words were crossed out before the entry continued.), *as naturally as a teacher. Then when Rose asked for a story about fairies he made one up just for her.*

*Ralph was enchanted by the girls, I think. I asked them to take a nap in their room after our picnic and they agreed — as long as Ralph would tell them one more story. When they were asleep Ralph and I sat in the kitchen and had tea. It was as if the years hadn't passed at all. Funny. Ralph is wounded — disfigured — and was sitting in my kitchen in a chair built by my husband, and still it was as if the years hadn't passed. I could look into his eyes and see the man who had said good-bye to me on the evening before he left for Europe.*

When Abby and Rose had awakened, their mother had told them it was time for Ralph to leave. *"Now, this must be our secret," I instructed them later. "Secrets are fun, aren't they? So this is our own fun secret."*

"Ralph is a secret?" Abby asked. She wanted to be sure.

"Yes. Ralph is a secret. His visit is a secret. Do you understand? We mustn't talk about his visit."

Then Abby surprised me. She said, "We mustn't talk about it in front of Pop, is that right?" She understands more than I give her credit for.

"Yes, that's right," I said.

And they kept the secret. My girls kept our secret.

# Chapter 13

*Sunday, May 25th, 2008*

"Georgia, what are you doing in there?"

It was Richard's voice.

"Nothing!" Georgia called through her closed bedroom door.

"But you've been in there all day."

Georgia looked at her watch. It was only 3:00 and Richard had only been home since lunchtime. How would he know how long she'd been in her room? "Do you want something?" she asked him.

"I want to know what you're doing."

"Reading."

"Oh." She heard his footsteps trail away. Then she heard the front door open and close.

Georgia set down Nell's journal and rubbed her eyes. Through her open window she could hear lazy crickets, the sound of a radio playing faintly (where? next door?), and the *whoosh, whoosh* of the ocean, which was ever-present in her life, so she rarely noticed it. It was like a heartbeat, necessary, dependable, relegated to the background.

Georgia knelt at the window and wondered how similar the scene was to the one that would have greeted Nell when she'd looked out the window. What had it looked like in 1919 when Nell and Luther had first moved here? There wouldn't have been any rosebushes in the garden then either. No need for them yet. What had the view looked like ten years later when Ralph had visited? What had it looked like when Nana Dana had lived here so briefly? Or when Georgia's mother had been a little girl and visited the cottage with her best friend, who grew up to become Georgia's aunt Kaycee? Georgia suspected that while the trees had grown, not much else had changed. The idea pleased her.

She resettled herself on her bed and picked up the third journal, curious to know if Nell and Ralph had seen each other again after their first secret visit. She wanted this for them desperately, all the while wondering if she was wrong to want it so badly.

*But surely they could just be friends, couldn't they?* Georgia wondered. *What would be wrong with a friendship?* But if they couldn't let Luther know about the relationship, then perhaps something *was* wrong. On the other hand, Luther seemed like the kind of person who wouldn't approve of his wife being friends with a man. After all, he didn't even want his wife to have friends who were women.

Georgia read on, hoping to see Ralph's name again. She didn't have to wait long. There were plenty of mentions of letters from Ralph.

*Heard from Ralph again!*

*Lovely, long letter from Ralph.*

And mentions of Nell's own letters to Ralph.

*Spent all morning writing to Ralph — ten pages! Who knew I had so much to say?*

At Christmastime in 1929, Nell had meticulously, lovingly, and privately made a card for him, working at odd moments when Abby and Rose were occupied and Luther was at work.

Nell was an artist, Georgia marveled, just like her granddaughter, Dana.

Time passed. The Great Depression descended on the country, although it didn't seem to change much for Nell's family. They had about the same amount of nothing once the Depression was underway as they'd had beforehand.

The communication between Nell and Ralph continued. In secret, of course. Sometimes, though, Georgia read for pages and pages without a mention of Ralph Saunders. The Nell who wrote those entries sounded much more like the other Nell. Gone was the buoyancy and effervescence. She sounded like the Nell of the final journal.

The entries wobbled between elation and despair. One day Nell would write: *Heard from Ralph again! His letters fill me with sweetness!* Three days later she would write: *Yesterday was another hard day. I fixed Luther his breakfast, but after he left the cottage, I went back to bed. I know it's wrong to leave Abby in charge of Rose, but I don't know what to do. My brain is muddled.*

Georgia realized that while Nell was able to keep Ralph a secret from Luther, she couldn't keep her confusion and sadness a secret from him. *Luther has asked me to control my spells. He says they're embarrassing.*

"Her spells," murmured Georgia. "That's what's embarrassing. That Luther says his wife has *spells.*"

The third journal came, depressingly, to an end, and after a trip to the kitchen for a plum and a glass of water, Georgia sat on her bed with journal number four. This one began in early 1930. Georgia drew in a breath and returned to Nell's story.

She read about dull days, and about chilly days as another Maine winter wore on. She read about washing clothes (by hand) and preparing endless meals for a family of four. Winter turned to spring, and then — at last — another letter from Ralph arrived.

*Too much to take in!* Nell wrote giddily. *Could we really do this? Could we really go away together? Even two days with Ralph would be heaven. But, but . . .*

Nell's words drifted off, and Georgia easily filled them in. But how would Nell and Ralph achieve this? How would they manage to go away together, right under Luther's nose? What would happen to Abby and Rose? What if Nell and Ralph got caught?

Georgia was almost breathless as she read on. She wanted desperately for Nell, who now seemed quite real to her, to have this moment in her life. A spotlight moment. The next entry was dated several weeks later, and Georgia could tell just by looking at it (it was peppered with exclamation points) that somehow the trip was going to take place.

The plans were in motion.

Georgia wished she could somehow have witnessed the events leading up to Nell and Ralph's weekend, but she had to satisfy herself with Nell's journal entries, some of which were maddeningly brief:

*I asked Luther if he thought I might have a short respite, just a little time away. I said I need to be by myself for a bit, that I need to gather my thoughts.* (Georgia didn't know what the answer to this had been.)

Another entry: *Betty has offered to take the girls for a few days.* (Did Betty know Nell's secret? Georgia wondered.)

The very next entry: *Two days in Owls Cove! I told Luther that Betty had mentioned the inn there. It's not fancy, but anyway Luther said never mind the expense. He's worried about my health, I can tell. Should I feel guilty? Maybe.*

*But I don't.*

And on a Friday a mere week later: *I leave this afternoon. Betty picked the girls up an hour ago. They're excited about their weekend with their cousins — their first weekend away without Luther or me. I expected a few tears, and got them, but only from Abby. Rose dashed into Betty's arms and hugged her, then climbed into the car without a glance back. Abby clung to me, even when I reminded her that she's the big sister and Rose will be looking up to her.*

*Now I wait. In two hours Luther will take me to the train station, and the dream will begin.*

This entry ended at the bottom of a page. Georgia turned it, expecting to see the next entry dated the following day, and was surprised to see that it was dated two weeks later. What had happened?

Only good things, as it turned out. Nell simply hadn't had much time to write, and, Georgia realized, probably hadn't brought her journal to Owls Cove. But the weekend had been a success. Luther hadn't discovered the true purpose of the trip. Far more important, Nell and Ralph had spent two idyllic days together. They'd checked into the inn as Eleanor Nichols and Robert Brown. Two separate rooms, and a fake name for Ralph, just in case Luther became suspicious about his wife's weekend of healing.

Nell wrote about *walking and dining with Ralph as if we were husband and wife.* Not near the inn, Georgia guessed, but elsewhere in the small town. *Time for talking and sharing, time for remembering and dreaming.*

Georgia thought the last part was sad, since what could Nell and Ralph reasonably dream about? Not a future together. Not children. Not any of the things Nell had once dreamed for them.

But Nell seemed happy anyway. Happier than she'd seemed at any time since Ralph's secret visit to the cottage in Lewisport.

*He's my soul,* Nell reported. *I have reconnected with my soul, and I feel whole again.*

Georgia felt tears spring to her eyes, and she swiped them away. If only Nell could have married Ralph, she thought. But if she had, there would have been no Great-Grandma Abby or Nana Dana or her mom or Georgia herself. Unless Nell had divorced Luther after her weekend with Ralph. But Georgia realized that was unlikely in 1931. Even if Luther had agreed to a divorce, he would never have given Nell custody of Abby and Rose.

And Abby and Rose were Nell's world. As happy as she had been to spend two days with Ralph — deliriously happy — she was just as happy to be reunited with her daughters.

*I was met with laughter and shrieks of joy when Betty and Marshall returned with the girls. Abby flew into my arms and Rose hugged me around my waist and wouldn't let go. I didn't want to let go either. We embraced and cried and laughed. Rose chattered about their adventures, and then I gave the girls the gifts I had bought: a red hair ribbon for Abby and a shell necklace for Rose. How good it feels to be in their presence again. They are my shining lights. They make the dull days brighter.*

Georgia read to the end of the fourth journal. Ralph was mentioned less frequently, and Georgia wondered if maybe, just maybe, Luther had become suspicious. One entry read: *Luther asked about Ralph this evening. He said, "Have you ever heard from Ralph Saunders?" An odd question since he thinks Ralph is dead. What happened?*

After that there were only two more mentions of Ralph in the fourth journal. And none, Georgia already knew, in the final journal. But for some reason she didn't feel sad. Nell had reconnected with her true love. They had met and communicated and he had made her happy. Georgia tried to let that outweigh what she knew had happened eventually.

She closed the fourth journal and glanced at the fifth. She looked at her watch. Almost six o'clock. She let out a sigh. Then she stacked the journals into a careful pile and set them in the hidey-hole. She replaced the piece of paneling and eyed it. She was certain no one would mistake it for anything other than a portion of the wall. Just in case, though, she tore the cover off of a magazine and hastily taped it over the panel. The picture was of the ocean, a scene so bland that Georgia was certain no one would be interested in it.

Georgia said good-bye to Nell.

It would be a year and a half before she would look at the journals again. And that time she would share them with someone.

# Chapter 14

*Thursday, September 10th, 2009*

Georgia stood on her front porch, eyes scanning Blue Harbor Lane for Mr. Norwood's car. It was the first day of high school and Ava's father was the driver of the morning carpool — Georgia, Ava, and Talia, but not Richard, who had announced over breakfast that he would no longer be part of it. His older friends could drive him.

Georgia's parents had protested, and Richard had ignored them. In fact, he had already left the house.

Behind her, Georgia heard the front door open and close.

"Are you nervous?" Henry asked her.

"No," said Georgia, who was so nervous she wondered if she was about to barf up her breakfast.

"But I heard that at the high school the big kids make the freshmen —"

"Stop!" cried Georgia. "I don't want to know."

"So you *are* nervous," said Henry, sitting on the top step and patting the space next to him.

Georgia sank down. She tried to calm her stomach.

The day before, she and Great-Grandma Abby had also sat on the porch, but in chairs, since Great-Grandma said her knees hadn't worked properly since 1982. And they had talked about high school.

"It's hard to believe that my own great-granddaughter is about to become a student at my alma mater." Great-Grandma shook her head.

(Neither of them mentioned that Richard was already a student there. His freshman year record had been far from stellar.)

"What was it like when you went to BPCHS?" Georgia had asked.

She and her great-grandmother were sitting in cushioned wicker chairs, drinking iced tea that Georgia had made with her own special process, which she would reveal to no one. She always worked behind closed doors.

"Well, the school seemed enormous, but it was actually smaller then than it is now," Great-Grandma replied. "The new addition in the back was put on about thirty years ago. I suppose some things aren't very different, though. We had graduation ceremonies and award ceremonies, and there were lots of clubs to join. On the other hand, even though there was no dress code, girls *always* wore dresses. We would never even have thought of wearing pants."

"Really?" asked Georgia, who rarely considered wearing anything other than jeans to school.

"Really." Great-Grandma smiled and sipped her iced tea. "This is wonderful. Would you share your recipe with me?"

"Nice try," said Georgia, grinning. "It's a secret from everyone. Great-Grandma, do you remember your first day at BPCHS?"

"I do."

"Were you nervous?"

"Not nervous, exactly."

"What then?"

Great-Grandma set down her glass and looked thoughtful. "It wasn't an easy time in my life."

"Were you afraid you wouldn't fit in with the other kids?"

"Is that what *you're* afraid of?"

Georgia nodded.

"Well, that was part of the problem," said Great-Grandma, "but I thought I wouldn't fit in because our family had so much money, and most of the students back then had very little. Our country was still recovering from the Depression.

And while we'd been poor at the start of it, we weren't by the end of it. My father had made a small fortune during the years of the Depression, which was almost unheard of."

"Oh. That's sort of the opposite of my problem. What was the rest of your problem?"

"You remember hearing about my friend Sarah, don't you?" asked Great-Grandma.

"The one who drowned?"

"Yes. The one who drowned. She'd died less than a year before, and everyone knew I'd been her best friend. My classmates tried to be nice to me after that, but eventually they just felt sorry for me. I became the girl whose friend had died tragically, and I found myself on the fringe of things by the time I started high school. But guess what."

"What?"

"There were so many more kids at BPCHS than there had been at my elementary school that most of my classmates didn't know anything about me. It was a chance to start over. Almost as if I'd moved to a new town."

*A chance to start over*, Georgia thought now as she sat with Henry. Maybe BPCHS could be her chance to start over. But Georgia wasn't sure. The kids who lived in Barnegat Point knew exactly which kids didn't live there. They knew which ones lived in Lewisport and St. George, towns a fraction the size of the much more sophisticated Barnegat Point. Never mind that Georgia and her friends had gone to elementary school in Barnegat Point. When the bell rang at the end of the day, their parents picked them up and drove them back to their little cottages and their little lives.

Georgia had a feeling this would make a difference in high school.

"There's Mr. Norwood's car," said Henry suddenly, and Georgia felt her stomach drop.

It was beginning.

When Mr. Norwood drove away from BPCHS, he left three uncertain girls standing at the edge of the front lawn with their backpacks. The school wasn't entirely foreign to them. They'd attended plays and concerts there, and just a week earlier, all the freshmen had been given a tour of the building. But Georgia could feel her heart pounding.

She glanced at Ava and Talia. "You guys look scared to death," she whispered.

"So do you," Talia whispered back.

"What do we have to be afraid of?" asked Ava suddenly, feeling brave.

"Lots of things," said Talia.

"Them," said Georgia, pointing to a group of much older kids sitting on a brick wall, laughing and punching one another and smoking.

Talia peered at them. "Isn't that Richard?" she asked, pointing to one of the boys.

Georgia sighed. "Yes."

"He could be your protector," said Ava.

Georgia didn't answer. Richard might or might not protect her. Either way, she was going to have to live down his reputation, which so far consisted of flunking courses, being given detention, frustrating his teachers, and disrupting the homecoming football game by leading his friends in a series of cheers for the opposing team.

Georgia planned to focus on her music and make her own kind of reputation. She looked at her friends. "Well, let's go."

If the girls had been any younger, they would have grabbed hands and walked across the lawn linked together. Instead they clutched their purses. Georgia clutched hers so tightly that her knuckles turned white.

They made their way past Richard and his friends, who paid them absolutely no attention, and entered the large double doors of the high school. Georgia was thinking about her conversation with Great-Grandma the day before, and feeling a pleasant sense of history, when Ava said, "Okay, now what?"

"What do you mean, 'Now what?'" asked Georgia, and was surprised to find that she was whispering again. She glanced around the crowded entryway, losing her footing when someone shoved her rudely aside.

"I mean," said Ava, who was also whispering, "now where do we go?"

Automatically, all three girls retrieved their schedules from their purses.

"We know what our classes are, but we don't know where the rooms are!" wailed Talia. "Where's Annex B-1?" She sounded near tears.

"Do not cry!" hissed Georgia.

"But this is like my nightmares," said Talia. "I'll probably wander around and around all day looking for classes and never finding any of them. And then I'll flunk out."

Georgia felt hysterical laughter bubbling to the surface, but she said, "We can't possibly be the only ones who don't know where their classrooms are. Look, there's Ginnie. Remember her? She's —"

At that moment Georgia felt a hand on her back and she nearly shrieked.

"Are you girls lost?" Richard was suddenly among them, and he was smiling. "I saw you go inside. I'll give you a piece of advice. Don't look so terrified."

"But we *are* terrified," said Georgia, as a guy wearing a leather jacket, his nose and lips pierced, brushed by her. He was at least a foot taller than Georgia and her friends.

"What's the problem?" asked Richard.

Georgia leaned close to him and whispered loudly, "We don't know where our classrooms are."

Richard smiled again. "Here. I'll help you."

And he did. He pointed each girl in the direction of her first class and told her how to get to her second one. Then he said to Georgia, "You'll probably want to sign up for band or something. All the sign-up sheets are posted in the hall by the principal's office, which is right down there."

Georgia looked at her brother as if he had floated into the halls of BPCHS in a giant bubble along with the Good Witch of the North. "Richard?"

He shook his head. "Don't say anything." He pulled out a packet of cigarettes and stuck one in his pocket. "See you."

Richard sauntered off — back through the double doors to the lawn, Georgia noticed — and she followed her brother's directions to her first class. She reached it unscathed.

Seven hours later, Georgia stood on the lawn of BPCHS with Ava and Talia.

"We survived," said Ava, laughing.

"I only got lost twice," said Talia.

"I signed up for two clubs," announced Georgia. "Band and theatre. And I'm going to try out for the talent show."

"There's Mom," said Talia, pointing. "She looks surprised to see us alive."

Georgia laughed. "Remember that I'm not going home with you. Richard and I are supposed to walk to Great-Grandma's old house today. I'll see you guys later."

Georgia watched the girls walk away and then looked around for her brother. She spotted him with his friends again. He appeared not to notice her, but crushed his cigarette beneath the heel of his sneaker, said, "See you," to a couple of boys, and materialized at Georgia's side.

"Okay, let's go."

Georgia and Richard walked off the BPCHS campus and through Barnegat Point to Haddon Road where, for several years, Great-Grandma had lived when she was young.

"I don't see the point of coming here," said Richard as he and Georgia climbed the steps to the grand old home. "It's just some rich person's house."

"You know why we're here," Georgia said. "Because the house is up for sale. Great-Grandma's stepmother died and we have to clear everything out. There might be something here you want. A memento or whatever."

"You mean like a china robin or a teacup or a photograph of some dog I don't know?"

Georgia laughed. "Be nice. Great-Grandma's here and this is probably hard for her. It was her home."

"It hasn't been her home for decades."

"Whatever. Just be nice."

Georgia knocked on the front door, tried the handle, found it unlocked, and let herself in. Richard followed sulkily. Inside they found their mother, Great-Grandma, and Henry. Her father was not there, having announced at breakfast that he had a house to show that afternoon — a teensy inland house, Georgia knew, but whatever.

Georgia looked around the living room (the parlor?) in awe, as she did every time she visited the house. It was hard to believe that people really lived like this, with so . . . much . . . of everything. With hired help to take care of the gardens and the cars, to cook meals, and even to take care of the children.

That was what Great-Grandma said life had been like in this house.

Now Georgia looked around at the room with its half-packed boxes and the furniture that was tagged to go to an auction house.

"What if we lived here?" she whispered to Richard.

He snorted. "Who wants all this?"

Georgia did. Sort of.

"The people from the auction house will be here tomorrow," Great-Grandma was saying. "So if there's anything you want, take it now."

Georgia watched her mother halfheartedly select an empty carton and eventually place a cast-iron parrot in it. "This fascinated me when I was little," she said. But when she let her eyes roam the room for another memento, they didn't land on anything else, and Georgia knew why. "I was never comfortable here," her mother had once told her. "Luther and Helen didn't really accept me." (Helen, Georgia knew, was Great-Grandma's stepmother, Luther's second wife.)

Great-Grandma stood and began to climb the stairs. "I just want to look in some of the rooms on the second floor," she said.

Georgia thought about Nell. Nell, who had lived in this house for just a few years before she'd died, a story only Georgia knew. She watched her great-grandmother reach the top step and begin the walk down the hall to the room

Luther had shared with Helen after Nell's death. Then she turned to her mother. "I think Great-Grandma needs a few moments to herself," she said.

Her mother didn't question this.

"So," said Richard. "We're supposed to take something?"

"If you want," Mrs. Noble replied.

"I want those," announced Henry, pointing to an old pair of spectacles.

"*Why?*" asked Richard.

"They look cool. Maybe I'll put them on and go back in time."

Georgia circled the room once, twice. Richard followed her.

"Anything?" their mother asked them.

"I guess not," said Georgia. "Is that rude?"

"Not at all."

"Let's go outside," said Richard.

Georgia and her big brother sat side by side on the top step of the veranda. The autumn sun shone down, turning the street golden.

"It's weird saying good-bye to something that wasn't yours to begin with," said Richard.

"Yeah." Georgia turned to look back at the house. "Actually, it's a relief."

Richard stared out at Haddon Road. Finally he said, "At school? If anyone gives you trouble? You can always come find me."

"Thanks," said Georgia.

Her brother withdrew a cigarette from his pocket, lit it, and puffed thoughtfully.

# Chapter 15

*Friday, December 11th, 2009*

Georgia stood at the living room window and looked out into the darkness of Blue Harbor Lane. Behind her, a fire blazed in the fireplace, and a little fir tree stood in the corner, not yet trimmed. Georgia could smell sugar and ginger and roast beef. She closed her eyes and thought of the gifts for her family that she had hidden under her bed, waiting to be wrapped and placed beneath the tree. She opened her eyes again and scanned the lane, searching for the first glimpse of headlights. At last she saw a gleam far to her right.

"I think they're here!" she called.

But the headlights turned into the driveway next door.

"Never mind," she said.

Henry joined her at the window. "When are they going to come? I can't wait any longer."

"You two have Christmas fever," their father called from the kitchen.

"Someone set the table for dinner, please. That will help the time pass," added their mother.

Georgia and Henry were rolling red Santa napkins into green holders, and arranging holly berry plates around the table, when a knock sounded on the door.

"It's them!" shrieked Henry. "They're here!"

Georgia abandoned the table and she and Henry flung the front door open. "Merry Christmas!" she cried.

Great-Grandma and Orrin were standing on the porch, flakes of snow sticking to their hats, their scarves, the shoulders of their overcoats. Orrin's arms were full of gifts.

"Merry Christmas!" called Georgia's parents from behind them.

"Merry Christmas!" said Great-Grandma and Orrin. They stepped inside.

"The tree isn't decorated yet, but you can put your presents under it anyway," said Henry, who was so excited that he was hopping from one foot to the other.

An early celebration with Great-Grandma and Orrin had been planned, since they were going to spend Christmas at an inn in Vermont that year, just the two of them. "It's our Christmas present to each other," Orrin had told the Nobles. (Henry had shot Georgia a look that plainly said, "That's it? No *real* presents?")

"Come in, come in," Georgia's father said now. "Let me take your coats."

"And I can take the presents," said Henry, holding his arms out.

"Where's Richard?" asked Great-Grandma.

"He'll be here," said Mrs. Noble, and everyone knew what that meant. He might or might not be there.

But just moments later, as Georgia and her family were settling before the fire, the door opened, and in strode Richard. "Hey," he said, kissing Great-Grandma and standing awkwardly in front of Orrin. "Um, happy holidays."

Henry wanted to open the presents immediately, but Georgia's parents insisted on dinner first.

"A real Christmas dinner," said Mr. Noble.

And it was. Roast beef, Yorkshire pudding, glazed carrots, and, for dessert, warm gingerbread topped with whipped cream.

Later, when everyone declared that they were stuffed and couldn't eat another bite, they sat before the fire again, the grown-ups drinking coffee and recalling Christmases long gone.

When he couldn't stand it any longer, Henry reached for a gift under the tree and said, "How about if I play Santa Claus?" He looked at the tag on the gift. "Great-Grandma, this one's for you from Mom and Dad." He handed the gift to his great-grandmother, and then began passing the rest of the presents around in a great rush. Soon everyone was tossing aside paper, exclaiming, laughing.

Georgia found herself with two gifts in her lap, and she opened them slowly. In a small box wrapped in red and tied with a gold ribbon she found a delicate silver necklace looped through a tiny G clef symbol.

"Oh, it's perfect!" she cried. "Thank you, Great-Grandma. Thank you, Orrin." The other gift, a bigger box, held a dark green leather-bound book, the word JOURNAL stamped in gold on the cover. Georgia laid it on her lap and stared at it.

Great-Grandma leaned close to her and whispered, "Georgia? Don't you like it?"

"Oh. I love it," said Georgia softly. "It's — it's great. Really."

Great-Grandma was frowning slightly. "Are you sure?"

"Yes, I — Great-Grandma? Could you come with me for a sec? I have to show you something." Georgia looked around at the rest of her family. They were examining their gifts, and her father was about to tell a story Georgia had heard at least a thousand times before. She knew she and her great-grandmother would not be missed. She rose, took

Great-Grandma's hand, and led her to her room, closing the door behind them.

Great-Grandma sat on the bed, looking puzzled. "What's the matter?" she asked.

"Nothing. I mean, nothing serious. Really. But I have to show you something. I probably should have shown you a long time ago, when I first discovered them —"

"Discovered . . . what?"

"These," said Georgia, removing the magazine cover from her wall.

Her great-grandmother watched in amazement as Georgia lifted the panel away and reached into the hole.

"What on earth?" Abby said.

"I discovered this hiding place a few years ago," Georgia confessed. "I didn't tell anyone about it." She withdrew the journals one at a time, all but the last one, and set them on the bed. "These were your mother's," she continued. "I should have told you about them, but I — I don't know — I kind of wanted a secret. I haven't shown them to anyone else," she added hurriedly. "Not Ava, not anyone. But I know you'll want to read them. At least, I think you will. There's kind of a big secret revealed in them. Something your mother did that might surprise you," said Georgia, recalling Nell's weekend with Ralph. "I hope you don't mind that I didn't share them right away."

Great-Grandma rested her hand on Georgia's. "Don't give it a second thought, honey. Just tell me everything. From the beginning."

Georgia sat beside her great-grandmother and related the story of the fight she'd had with Richard and her accidental discovery of the hiding place. "And the journals were in there," she said, pointing toward the wall. "I suppose they've been there since you were a little girl. I don't know how Nell discovered that the paneling would come away like that, but she discovered it sometime, and she kept it a secret."

"Have you read the journals?" asked Great-Grandma.

Georgia lowered her head. "Yes. I couldn't help it."

"And you discovered something about my mother?"

"Yes," Georgia said again, and felt her cheeks flush. She had discovered two secrets, but she wasn't prepared to ruin Great-Grandma's Christmas by revealing the second one.

"Do you want to tell me about it?"

Georgia squirmed. "Don't you want to read it yourself?"

"Well, eventually. But I think it will take me a while to get through these." Great-Grandma waved her hand above the four journals. Then she raised her eyebrows at Georgia.

Georgia continued to squirm.

"Is it an embarrassing secret?"

"Not really. It's surprising. But in the end I decided it was good. I think you'll like it. What — what do you remember about your mother?"

Great-Grandma looked thoughtful. "She was a wonderful mother. That's what I remember most. But she was also unhappy. I suppose today we would say she was depressed, but back then we didn't have much understanding of things like that. She was sad about the babies . . ." Great-Grandma's eyes drifted out Georgia's window to the dark garden.

"There was something else," said Georgia. "Your father wasn't . . . wasn't her true love."

Great-Grandma looked startled. "What?"

"He wasn't her true love. She had loved someone else, a boy named Ralph who she had known since they were kids. But Ralph's plane was shot down in World War One and everyone thought he was dead, so when your father came along, your mother married him. It's all in the journals," Georgia added. "Anyway, it turned out that Ralph hadn't died after all, and years later, when your mother was married and you and Rose were little, she heard from him. They started writing to each other and even saw each other a couple of times. He made your mom very happy." Georgia had been speaking at high speed, trying to give her great-grandmother all the details she remembered from the journals, but now she came to a stop as she watched Great-Grandma's expression change from one of puzzlement to one of awe.

"Georgia, what did you say this man's name was?"

"Ralph," Georgia replied. "Ralph Saunders."

"Well, my goodness." Great-Grandma put her hand to her mouth.

"Are you okay?"

Great-Grandma shook her head, but she was smiling. "My goodness," she said again.

# Chapter 16

*Friday, December 11th, 2009*

## Abigail Nichols Umhay

The memory came back to Abby in a rush, almost like a flash of light. One moment she was sitting on Georgia's bed hearing about her mother's secret life, and the next moment the tiny room had disappeared, along with Georgia and the nighttime and the scent of Christmas.

Abby was six years old, standing at the front door of the cottage on a sunny summer day, holding Rose's hand, waiting expectantly. Her father wasn't there, but then he wasn't usually at home during the day, except maybe on Sunday. He was away in Portland, Abby remembered. And she and Rose were dressed in their very best dresses, the ones that matched, the ones their mother had sewn for them in a burst of energy a few days earlier.

"Now I want you to be on your best behavior," their mother had just said to them. "This is a special guest. His name is Ralph, and you're to be very, very nice to him. He's an old friend. He was wounded in the war, so you mustn't say anything about his face."

"What's wrong with his face?" Rose had asked immediately.

"It's scarred," their mother had replied. "And you don't want to embarrass him, so please just shake his hand and say, 'How do you do?' and be polite. All right? All right, *Rose*?"

"All *right*. But I'll have to look at his face, won't I? I'm supposed to look at his face when I shake his hand. That's what you always say."

"Yes, you may look at his face. Just don't comment on it."

A picnic had been promised when Ralph arrived. A picnic in the backyard. Abby was excited. She longed to tell her friend Sarah about the unexpected treat, but her mother had said something else. She had said they must not talk about the visit.

Now Abby stood nervously at the door to the cottage, holding her sister's hand and watching the road. Soon enough a car chugged to a stop on Blue Harbor Lane, and a man got out and walked quickly to the front door. He stopped when he saw Abby and Rose on the other side of the door, trying not to stare at his face, but too fascinated to look away.

It wasn't a horrible face, Abby thought. But the skin on one side was pitted and pulled and stretched like a piece of taffy. And the eye on that side drooped.

For a moment, Ralph looked in at the girls and the girls looked out at him. Finally Abby called over her shoulder, "Mama, he's here!" and the special day began. It was filled with stories and lemonade and tomato sandwiches and games and more stories. Abby forgot about Ralph's face. He was kind and let her climb into his lap. He answered her questions and asked questions of his own, but they weren't the usual questions grown-ups asked. Ralph didn't want to know about school or what Abby's favorite food was. Instead he asked what the best day of her life had been, and what she thought was the greatest modern invention. Then he and Abby and Rose and Mama had made up a game about animals, and Abby saw her mother laugh harder than ever before.

When it came time for Ralph to leave, Abby had hugged him and Rose had cried a little. After that, as they watched his funny car chug away, their mother had again cautioned them about secrets. She had said that the visit was a secret and so was Ralph. Suddenly Abby had understood. Ralph and the visit were a secret from Pop more than from anyone else.

She wasn't sure why. But she saw that her mother was happy and she didn't want to spoil that.

Neither she nor Rose mentioned Ralph or the wonderful day of the picnic and stories and games. As they grew older, the memory faded anyway, as so many other things happened. The Nicholses moved out of the cottage, and later Mama died, and Abby grew up and moved to New York and had a family of her own.

And now here she was in the cottage again, sitting with her great-granddaughter, who had just given her the best gift ever, the lost memory of a happy day.

"Great-Grandma?" said Georgia. "Here. You should take the journals. You'll probably want to read them in order, like I did." Georgia set the four journals in her great-grandmother's lap.

"Yes," Abby said. "I want to read every word."

"I guess you'll want to keep them."

"I don't know. It seems to me that the journals belong here, where my mother left them. I'll bring them back after the holidays."

"Maybe the journals should be our secret," said Georgia. "I don't know why, but I don't feel like sharing them with anyone else. Not yet."

Abby considered her great-granddaughter, whose gaze kept returning to the hiding place in the wall. "Hmm," she said. "All right. They can be a secret for now, okay?"

"Okay." Georgia rose and replaced the panel, then taped the magazine cover over it again.

Abby held out her hand. "Come," she said.

Together they left the bedroom and joined the others by the fire.

# Chapter 17

*Tuesday, June 22nd, 2010*

Georgia sat on the bottom step of the front stoop and stretched her bare legs in front of her so that they pointed across Blue Harbor Lane to the ocean that was growing gray in the twilight. She rested her back uncomfortably on the step behind her and breathed in the humid air. The day had been hot and muggy, and everything she touched felt wet, including her hair, which had turned into an astonishing mass of curls.

Behind her, the door to the porch opened and closed, and a moment later Henry sat down beside her. "Seventy-nine days of summer vacation left," he announced lazily.

Georgia smiled. This was the first year she hadn't bothered to count how many days of summer vacation lay ahead. When she was younger she had sometimes made a chart the day after school had ended so that she could see just how much freedom — how many days of ice cream and guitar playing and games with Ava and Talia and Penny —

stretched in front of her. (Often, though, she scrunched up the chart near the beginning of August as the days began to dwindle and September was closer than June had been.)

This year she hadn't even thought about a chart. She was eager for summer vacation, but she was just as eager to begin her sophomore year at BPCHS. This had come as a surprise to her — the realization that ninth grade had not been the disaster she'd feared and that tenth grade might be even better. Georgia had enjoyed her first year of high school. Her grades had been excellent and she'd made the honor roll. She'd made new friends, too; she'd joined both of the clubs that had caught her attention on the first day of school; and she'd put together a solo guitar performance for the talent show that had earned her the one and only standing ovation of the evening. Her private lessons with Mr. Elden had continued, and at the end of a recent one he'd exclaimed, "Georgia, I don't think I have anything left to teach you!" She hoped that wasn't true. She couldn't imagine Tuesday afternoons and Saturday mornings without her guitar and her sheet music and Mr. Elden's enthusiastic encouragement.

Henry stretched out his own legs, which, Georgia suddenly noticed, were nearly as long as hers. "Want to walk into town and get ice cream?" he asked.

"Maybe." Georgia was feeling particularly lazy. She'd spent the day babysitting for a new family down the lane. This was to be her summer job — sitting for the Harrison girls three days a week — and Georgia hadn't realized just how much energy a three-year-old, a five-year-old, and a six-year-old had, even in the heat.

Behind her, the door opened and closed again. Georgia and Henry's parents joined them on the stoop, cups of coffee in their hands.

"How can you drink hot coffee in this weather?" asked Georgia, brushing her sweaty hair back from her face.

"It's a ritual," said her father, and Georgia turned around in time to see him smile at her mother.

Her parents had seemed happier lately, she thought. Not much had changed that she could see. Her father still sold real estate spottily and still talked about starting a business that would one day make them rich, and her mother still wrote her novels that sold well but not spectacularly. Yet something had changed. Some adult thing, Georgia thought, and she didn't want to question it. They'd had a good, calm year, there had been barely any fighting, and her father had stayed put. That was enough for Georgia.

"Where's Richard?" asked Mrs. Noble.

Georgia leaned her head back and rested it on her mother's knees. "He left with Seth a little while ago.

"Seth? Seth who?"

"I don't know his last name. That new guy."

Mr. Noble looked at the driveway. "Well, they didn't take one of our cars."

"Nope. Seth was driving."

They sat quietly for a few minutes, listening to the ocean, the calls of the gulls, shouts from down the street where a group of kids were playing basketball.

"Don't you want to play with them?" Mr. Noble asked Henry, inclining his head in the direction of the game.

Henry shook his head. "Not tonight. This is nice. I don't even want ice cream anymore."

The phone rang then and Georgia's father jumped up and ran inside. He was carrying the cordless phone back to the porch when Georgia heard him say, "What? . . . *What?* . . . Is he okay?"

His voice was so sharp that Georgia, Henry, and their mother all turned to look up at him. Georgia could tell that her father had been about to sit on the stoop again, but now he remained standing, and his face became hard and tight.

"What is it?" cried Mrs. Noble, getting to her feet.

Georgia's father waved his hand at her. "Is he okay?" he asked again. "Please tell me he's okay."

Georgia looked at Henry in alarm. They jumped to their feet, too.

"We'll be right there," said Mr. Noble. He clicked off the phone. "There's been an accident," he said, hurrying back into the cottage. "Richard and his friends were in a car accident. That was the hospital. They wouldn't give me any more information."

"Who wouldn't?" asked Mrs. Noble. She grabbed her purse from the table by the door.

"Does it matter? I don't know who I was speaking to. But the accident sounds bad." Georgia's father was scrambling to find his wallet, the car keys.

"I'm coming, too," said Georgia.

"So am I," said Henry.

"No, you're not," said both of their parents.

"Yes, we are." Georgia slammed the cottage door behind her, vaguely aware of lights on, the radio in the kitchen playing softly. She jumped into the backseat of the Subaru, and Henry threw himself in next to her. Two minutes later they were on the road to Barnegat Point.

\*     \*     \*

Mr. Noble brought the Subaru to a screeching halt in the lot at the medical center. "Go inside and find Richard," he said breathlessly. "I'll be there as soon as I find a parking space."

Three car doors slammed behind Georgia, Henry, and their mother, and they ran through the emergency entrance. Mrs. Noble looked wildly around the crowded waiting room and spotted a young man sitting at a desk. She bolted toward him. "My son!" she cried. "My son was brought in. A car accident. His name is Richard Noble. Where is he?"

"He's being taken care of. He —"

"I want to see him!"

"Someone will help you in just a moment."

"I want to see him now!"

"Mom," said Georgia, tugging on her mother's arm.

"Ma'am, you'll have to wait," said the man.

"No, he's my son!" Georgia's mother paused. "He's alive, isn't he? Say he's alive."

"Yes, he's alive. They're working on him. I need to get someone who can take you to him. Please have a seat."

Mrs. Noble couldn't sit. She remained standing at the desk and was still there when Georgia's father hurried through the doors. A moment later, a nurse appeared. "I'll take you back," he said.

"Us, too?" asked Georgia.

The nurse shook his head. "Parents only."

Georgia and Henry sat in orange plastic chairs that hurt their backs, and watched the activity in the waiting room. A man and a woman arrived in a big hurry and ran to the desk. "We're here about the accident," said the man. "Our son — his name is Seth — they wouldn't give us any information over the phone."

Georgia glanced at Henry.

Another couple arrived, the woman crying. The waiting room now seemed frantic to Georgia. The lights were too bright, and the noise level was rising.

Georgia drew up her knees and buried her face in them. She and Henry sat nearly motionless, not speaking, until after what seemed like hours she felt a gentle hand on her shoulder. She raised her head and looked into her father's eyes.

"He's going to be okay," he said. "Come with me. One of the doctors will talk to us now."

Georgia, Henry, and their parents were taken into a small room. A doctor (who looked, Georgia thought, unbearably tired) followed them, and they all perched on the edges of chairs.

"Okay," the doctor began, "it was a bad accident, but Richard was lucky. As you know," she went on, turning to Georgia's parents, "he fractured his thigh and he'll need surgery to repair it. He has a mild concussion, too, and lots of cuts. Some required stitches. I expect he'll be in the hospital for at least a week."

"That's lucky?" said Henry.

Georgia saw her parents glance at each other. "Kids," said their father, "the truth is that Richard and his friends had been drinking, and — there's no easy way to tell you this — the two boys who were in the car with Richard were killed. They hit another car head-on."

Henry's eyes widened, but he said nothing.

"What about the people in the other car?" whispered Georgia. "Are they okay?"

The doctor said quietly, "There was just one person in the other car, and he didn't make it either."

Georgia felt the room spinning around her and she gripped the arms of her chair. "Oh no. Oh no," she moaned.

It was her mother who spoke next. "We have to be strong," she said firmly. "This is not the time to fall apart. Richard needs us now."

"But three people. Dead," said Georgia.

"Richard is going to have to live with this for the rest of his life," her father said.

"Why would he let a drunk person drive the car he was in?" asked Henry.

*171*

Mrs. Noble shook her head. "This isn't the time for blame either," she replied. "Let's focus on Richard. He has a long recovery ahead of him. Emotional as well as physical."

"What happens now?" Mr. Noble asked the doctor.

"We'd like to do the surgery first thing in the morning. We're calling in a specialist from Bangor, someone who has more experience with this kind of fracture than the orthopedic surgeons here do. Richard is sedated now and he'll sleep through the night. I suggest you go home and get some sleep, too."

The Nobles, exhausted, followed the doctor back to the waiting room, where Georgia spotted a clock on the wall behind the desk and was astonished to realize it was after midnight. Blearily, she and her family climbed into their car and drove slowly back to the cottage.

Georgia awoke the next morning to sunlight streaming through her windows. She had forgotten to pull the blinds down after she'd returned from the hospital. She hadn't taken her clothes off either, or even brushed her teeth.

She sat up and rubbed her eyes, listening to the sound of the radio playing in the kitchen, then stumbled out of her room and found her mother sitting at the table with a cup of coffee. "I thought you'd already be at the hospital," she said.

"Your dad's there," Mrs. Noble replied. "I wanted to talk to you before I go back."

Georgia sat across from her mother, feeling her heart begin to pound. "Talk to me about what? Richard's still going to be okay, isn't he?"

"Yes." Mrs. Noble's voice caught in her throat. "It's something else. It's about the driver of the other car." She opened her arms. "Come sit with me, honey."

Georgia didn't say, "I'm too big for your lap." She got up woodenly, heart pounding even harder, and sat on her mother's knees, feeling strong arms wrap around her.

"The other driver," said Mrs. Noble. "I'm so sorry, Georgia, but the other driver was Mr. Elden."

Georgia felt her world melt away.

# Chapter 18

*Thursday, November 25th, 2010*

"Are we the only family in America who isn't having turkey today?" Henry asked Georgia. He was slumped on the couch in front of the television, the last moments of the Macy's Thanksgiving Day parade playing on mute.

Georgia made a face at her brother. "You know, lots of families can't even *afford* a turkey. Don't be such a brat."

Henry turned to Georgia with wounded eyes. "Why are you being so mean?"

"Why are you being such a baby?"

"I thought you said I was a brat."

"Maybe you're both."

"Georgia? Could I see you in the kitchen for a moment, please?" called their mother.

"Ha, ha. Now you're in trouble," said Henry, but he didn't sound particularly happy about it.

Georgia heaved herself off the couch, made her way droopily into the kitchen, and slumped in a chair. Her mother was at the stove, dropping handfuls of pasta into a pot of boiling water. Georgia sniffed the air and caught the scent of oregano, but nothing that reminded her even remotely of past Thanksgivings. In fact, she realized, there was nothing in the house that spoke of the holiday, except for the parade playing silently on the television.

"What?" said Georgia.

"I might ask the same of you," replied her mother. "Except that I'd do it a bit more politely. What is going on? Why are you being so mean to Henry?"

Georgia was about to say, "Because he's behaving like a brat," but thought better of it. "I don't know," she said instead, which was mostly true. She felt as though she'd been in a bad mood for months — since the night of the accident — but she didn't know why she was taking it out on Henry.

"Could you please try to express your feelings?" asked Mrs. Noble, turning away from the stove to look at her daughter.

Georgia studied her mother's face, which was lined and worn and pale. She wanted to say, "Could *you* please try to express *your* feelings?" but she didn't feel like having a conversation about anyone's feelings. "No," she said, and left the kitchen.

"Don't slam your door!" called her father from upstairs.

*How did he even know what was going on?* wondered Georgia. She closed her door as loudly as she could without being accused of slamming it.

She lay on her bed, hands behind her head, stared at the ceiling, and thought about the dreary Thanksgiving. They could have had a perfectly nice Thanksgiving, except that no one in her family, including Georgia herself, seemed to care much about the holiday. Not even Henry. Henry wanted turkey, but that was it.

Her thoughts shifted to the accident, five months earlier. She felt as though everything Richard had done in his life had led directly to that night, to the accident, to the deaths of his friends and of Mr. Elden. His bad behavior, sneaking around, defying their parents, drinking, probably doing drugs (although Georgia didn't have any evidence of that) — all those things had created a trail like a path on the Candy Land board that led to his climbing into a car with a boy who was already drunk, and then to start drinking himself. He continued hopping along the path from one square to the next until he found that the car in which he was riding was careening across the center line of a back road and plowing into a car driven by an unsuspecting, perfectly sober music teacher. And he survived, while everyone else died.

It would have been worse, far worse, Georgia knew, if

Richard had been the driver. She couldn't imagine how Seth's parents felt, losing their son *and* knowing what he had caused. She also knew that Seth wasn't the only one at fault.

Around and around went Georgia's thoughts. She couldn't count the number of nights she had lain in bed since June, thinking these exact same things. In those months she had attended Mr. Elden's funeral, sitting not up front with the rest of his students, but in the back with her family — her parents and Henry, but not Richard because he was still in the hospital — and feeling like a pariah. In fact, Penny and Talia, who had loved Mr. Elden, had been frosty to Georgia for weeks following the accident, as if she, not Richard, had been in the car.

In those months Georgia had watched Richard struggle with his physical therapy, and, to her surprise, take it seriously, push his limits, and exceed what his doctors had predicted. He had stayed close to home and dropped most of his old friends. When school had started, he'd quietly tackled his classes, taking his courses as seriously as he took his physical therapy. Georgia was pleased that Richard seemed to have turned around, but why had it happened at Mr. Elden's expense?

In those months, Georgia had not once picked up her guitar. It stood in its case in a corner of her room. She looked at it from time to time, curiously, as though it were an insect she hadn't seen before, but without enough interest to investigate further.

"We can find you another teacher," her father had offered.

"Why don't you at least practice?" her mother had asked. "Plan something for the next talent show."

"That's okay," Georgia had said to both of them.

Her father hadn't sold a house in months. Her mother didn't have an idea for her next book. The Nobles, it seemed, were stalled. Except for Richard, who plowed ahead with his schoolwork and his therapy.

Now here it was Thanksgiving Day and Georgia's family had planned a spaghetti dinner for the afternoon, just the five of them. Nobody felt like celebrating.

The doorbell rang.

"I'll get it!" Georgia heard Henry call. "It's probably the Quigley boys."

"On Thanksgiving?" said her father. His voice sounded nearby, and Georgia realized he must have come downstairs. She looked at her watch. She'd been lying on her bed stewing (as her mother would say) for over an hour.

The next sound Georgia heard was a shriek. Not a frightened shriek, but a surprised and happy one. And then she heard Henry cry, "Nana Dana!"

Nana Dana? Here?

Georgia heard more shouting and laughter, and finally she couldn't stand it any longer. She rose from her bed and opened her door.

"There she is!" exclaimed her grandmother.

Nana Dana was still wearing her coat, a large cloth coat, and when she turned to Georgia and opened her arms, the sleeves fanned out like bat wings.

Georgia couldn't help smiling. She ran to her grandmother and threw herself against her. "I didn't know you were coming," she managed to say.

"Of course not. None of you did. That's why this is such a good surprise. I thought you needed a surprise, and a little holiday cheer."

The door to Richard and Henry's room opened then, and Richard limped out, his eyes bleary.

Nana Dana stood back from Georgia and watched Richard cross the room. "My goodness," she said at last. "You look terrible."

There was a moment of silence, and then Richard grinned. "I have a paper due on Monday."

"And you've been working on Thanksgiving?"

"Yup."

Georgia saw her parents smile at each other.

"Well, for heaven's sake," said her mother after a moment. "Take your coat off, Dana. What's all that?" She indicated the shopping bags at Nana Dana's feet. "And how on earth did you get here?"

"Train," replied Nana Dana. "And a cab. And all that," she said, "is food from the Big Apple. I intend for you to have a proper Thanksgiving feast. Well, maybe not a proper one, but a feast at any rate. I understand," she went on, glancing at Henry, "that you're somewhat lacking in Thanksgiving spirit around here."

Henry blushed slightly. But then he said, "What did you bring?"

Nana Dana smiled at him. "I couldn't bring a turkey on the train, but there's canned turkey and, well, go ahead and open the bags."

Henry dove for them, followed by Richard and Georgia.

"Bagels!" cried Georgia holding a cardboard box aloft.

"Oil-cured olives," said Richard, squinting at the label on a plastic container.

"Like I said, it might not be a traditional Thanksgiving dinner," said Nana Dana. "But it will be festive."

"It will be better than spaghetti," said Henry, examining a box of chocolate-covered marzipan candies.

\*　　\*　　\*

At 3:00 that afternoon, the Nobles and Nana Dana gathered around the kitchen table, which was covered with a red cloth and set for six people. A chocolate turkey stood by each water glass, and Georgia had even made place cards, just as she used to do when she was a little girl.

"Serve yourselves from the counter," said Georgia's mother. "Let Nana Dana go first."

Georgia looked at the array of food: canned turkey, bagels and lox, Chinese noodles, a vegetable she couldn't identify but wanted to try anyway, curried lentil soup, the olives, and at the far end of the counter, the pot of spaghetti.

When everyone was seated and looking longingly at their plates, Nana Dana said, "Before we start eating, I'd like for each one of us to say what we're thankful for. Henry, you go first."

Georgia looked around the table and saw lowered eyes and fidgeting hands, but Nana Dana was serious about her request.

"Um, okay, well, I'm thankful you brought all this food here and we don't have to have a spaghetti dinner," said Henry.

Nana Dana smiled. "Georgia?"

Georgia stared out the window. "I don't know."

Her grandmother eyed her. "You aren't thankful about anything?"

"I don't know."

"Nothing at all?"

"Okay. I'm thankful you're here."

"All right. Richard?"

"I — well, I'm thankful *I'm* here. And I'm not being funny."

Silence. Then Georgia's father said, "It may not have been the best year —"

"I'll say," muttered Georgia.

"Excuse me. Georgia? You had your turn to speak," said Nana Dana. "Now it's your father's turn."

"Sorry."

"It may not have been the best year," Georgia's father said again, "but we survived it, we're all here, together, and Richard is getting healthy again. That's a pretty big gift."

"Francie?" said Nana Dana, turning to Georgia's mother.

"We got Richard back. We got him back."

"Now you," said Henry, looking at his grandmother.

"I'm thankful to be sitting at a table with the people I love best in the world. All right. Dig in, everybody."

Georgia watched her family. Henry stuffed four olives into his mouth. Richard reached for the cream cheese and said, "Do you think the Pilgrims ate lox and bagels?" Georgia's mother dropped a roll on the floor and Nana Dana picked it up and lobbed it across the kitchen, directly into the garbage pail. Georgia's father began to laugh.

Nana Dana turned to Georgia. "Aren't you going to eat?"

Suddenly Georgia smiled. "Yup," she said, reaching for her fork. "I am. But while we eat, could we tell Thanksgiving stories? Like the year your turkey caught on fire?"

"Haven't you heard that a zillion times?"

"Yes, but I want to hear it again."

"Will you tell Great-Grandma's story about the Thanksgiving blizzard in the olden days?" asked Henry.

So the stories began. Georgia sat with her family around the table in the kitchen, eating strange food from New York City, and watching the light fade outside until her mother had to get up to turn on the lamps.

# Chapter 19

Georgia stood for a moment with her hand on the knob of her bedroom door. She took two deep breaths and let them out slowly. Breath in, breath out, breath in, breath out. She was going to have to play the breakfast conversation very, very carefully.

She opened her door.

Then she adjusted the strap of her guitar and headed for the kitchen.

"Morning, everyone," she said.

"Morning, Georgie Girl," replied her mother.

"Guitar lesson this afternoon?" asked her father.

"Yup," said Georgia. She set her guitar and books on the couch in the living room, then returned to the kitchen and took her place at the table.

"Why does Mrs. Windham give us *so* much homework?" Henry was moaning. "She's so mean. And so unfair."

"You have to spread yourself out," Richard told him. "Don't save everything for the last minute. If you do, then you'll have to finish all your work in a clump."

"Unh," grunted Henry. "I guess."

He took a bite of cereal so enormous that Georgia was tempted to ask him why he didn't just use a ladle, but she held her tongue. She needed her parents' approval this morning.

"Guess what," said Georgia brightly. She put on a smile and looked around at each member of her family.

"What?" said Richard, and it occurred to Georgia that she should have enlisted her brother to help her in this venture, but it was too late. She needed to give Natalie and the other girls an answer before school ended that day.

"It's the best thing," Georgia went on. She glanced at the clock and saw that she had only ten minutes before she and her brothers would have to leave for school. Perfect. She wanted to rush her parents into a decision, not give them too much time to mull things over — or for her mother to list eight million reasons why Georgia shouldn't be allowed to take advantage of the best opportunity that had come her way in years.

"What is it, sweetie?" asked her mother.

"Okay. Well, you know Natalie Lauck?"

"That senior?" interrupted Richard. "She's hot."

"Ahem," said Mr. Noble.

"Let me speak, please," said Georgia, and then caught herself. She didn't want any accusations about her tone of voice. "Yes, she's a senior," she said carefully, "and she and her friends have a band."

"Hot Chix," said Richard. "Which is why I called her hot. But how come the band is called Hot Chix when there are boys in it?"

"There's only one boy," Georgia replied. "He plays bass, sort of in the background. The lead singers are three girls, and they started the band. *Anyway*, they have, um, a gig. In Bar Harbor this weekend. One of their guitar players can't go with them and they asked me to fill in. So can I? Please?"

Henry suddenly looked interested. "You want to go on a road trip?"

Georgia glared at him. "I want to help them out. Being asked to fill in is a really big honor. They're all seniors, but they know me because they've heard me play in the talent shows. It would be a great experience for me. Musically."

"Honey, that's wonderful," said her father.

"Who's driving?" her mother wanted to know.

"I don't know."

"One of their parents?"

"No, I don't think any parents will be going along."

"So one of the kids will be driving?" asked her mother, just as her father asked, "When is the show?"

"Saturday night."

"So when would you be home?"

"I don't know exactly. If it's really late we might spend the night there and come home on Sunday."

"No," Mrs. Noble said firmly.

"What?" said Georgia.

"No. I don't want you riding around with a bunch of kids —"

"They're eighteen."

"All right, with a bunch of eighteen-year-olds, and spending the night in some strange place. You're only sixteen, Georgia."

"And I've never been in trouble! I get straight As, I'm on the honor roll, I found a new guitar teacher all by myself, and I pay for my own lessons now —"

"I'm not saying you aren't responsible," her mother continued. "But I don't know how responsible those other kids are. They're eighteen. They could do a lot of stupid things."

"Are you saying they're too old or too young?"

"Georgia," said her mother.

"But seriously!" Georgia slammed her hands on the table and stood up so fast that her chair skidded away from her and shot into the wall.

"Seriously, what?" asked Henry, looking from his sister to his parents.

"Seriously, I should be allowed to go."

"You're not making a very good case," said Mrs. Noble quietly.

"I *was* making a good case. You're just being overprotective. As usual."

"I think she should go," said Georgia's father.

"Absolutely not." Georgia's mother stood and began to clear the table. "Case closed. It's time for you to leave for school."

Georgia could feel her face burning. "But Mom!" She pictured Natalie Lauck and tried to envision telling her that she wasn't allowed to go. It would be like turning up for a field trip and saying that her mother wouldn't sign her permission slip and she'd have to stay behind and spend the day with the librarian.

"I said case closed."

"Talk about unfair." Georgia didn't bother to lower her voice. There was no point. She'd lost the battle.

"You could be in an accident," said her mother. "I'm not about to have another one of my children involved in a car accident."

"Mr. Elden was in a car accident, and he was an adult. A sober adult. Accidents can happen to anyone, any time. That's the definition of an accident."

This time her mother didn't reply, and just like that Georgia made a decision. It wasn't something she'd thought of before, it wasn't something she'd planned. But the idea came to her now, fully formed. She left the kitchen, went into her room, closing the door behind her, and grabbed a small duffel bag from her closet.

Why wouldn't her mother trust her? Georgia had made only good decisions, done only the right things. All her life. (Mostly.) She'd been the perfect daughter, the perfect sister, the perfect student. And what was her reward? A concert of denial. A festival of mistrust.

Georgia stuffed underwear and some random clothing into the duffel. Then she plunged her hand into the back of her bottom desk drawer and retrieved the wad of cash she'd been saving. She put it into an empty makeup bag and zipped the bag into a compartment of the duffel.

She patted Noelle and bounced out of her room. "Ready," she announced.

Her father and brothers were waiting at the front door. Georgia retrieved her guitar and backpack and joined them. "Bye," she called cheerfully to her mother.

Mrs. Noble smiled at her. "You'll see that you've made the right decision," she said.

"Sure. Bye."

Georgia's father dropped Henry at the middle school, and let Richard and Georgia out in front of the high school. Georgia looked at her older brother as their father drove away. "You go ahead," she told him. "I'm going to wait here for Ava." Richard loped off. Georgia watched until he had disappeared through the front doors. Then she turned and walked into town.

An hour later she was sitting on a Greyhound bus, Barnegat Point sliding away behind her.

She reached Nana Dana's apartment building at seven thirty that evening. Most of her cash was gone, fifteen dollars having recently been spent on a cab from the Port Authority to the Upper West Side after Georgia decided she was too nervous to try to figure out the subway system.

"I'm here to see Dana Goldberg," she said to the doorman. "I'm her granddaughter."

"Just a moment," he replied. He spoke into a phone, then turned to her and said, "Go on up. Fourth floor. Apartment D."

When the elevator doors opened on the fourth floor, Georgia found herself facing her grandmother, who was crying.

"Georgia!" exclaimed Nana Dana. "What on earth!" She hauled her out of the elevator and into the hallway. "I should turn you over my knee," she went on, but then she drew Georgia into a tight hug. "Do you know what your parents are going through?"

Georgia followed her grandmother down the hall and into her apartment. She had a feeling that Nana Dana and her parents had already spoken. Probably many times that day. She had purposely not checked her phone for messages, not wanting to be tempted to turn around and go home.

"They've been worried sick."

"Did Mom tell you what happened this morning?"

Nana Dana sighed, then sank into an armchair. "Yes. But I'd like to hear your version of the story." She paused. "Are you hungry? Have you been traveling all day? How did you get here? You must be starved. Let me fix you something. I'll make you a sandwich while you call your parents."

"*What?* I'm not calling them."

"Oh, yes, you are. Right this minute. You tell them that you're okay and that you're here with me. They've already called the police."

"I'm not calling them," said Georgia flatly.

"Fine. I'll call them."

"Before you hear what happened?"

"Georgia. You weren't in school today. No one has heard from you since this morning. Yes, of course I'm going to call your parents. That's the end of this discussion."

Dana Burley Goldberg had a brief conversation with Georgia's parents. Then she clicked off the phone and, with her back to Georgia, began to make a sandwich. "I want to hear what happened," she told her granddaughter. "We can stay up all night talking about it, if need be. Then I'm going to take you home."

"Tomorrow?"

"Maybe not tomorrow. But in a couple of days."

Georgia let out a prolonged sigh.

"Go put your things in the spare room," said Nana Dana. "Wash up. Then come back out here, eat your sandwich, and tell me what happened."

Georgia did as she was told. She related the morning's events and wound up by saying, "It's so unfair! I do everything right. I'm not like Richard. I do *everything* right, and Mom never trusts me. Never. I can't take it anymore."

"Which is exactly why you're going to go back home. I don't want you and your mother to end up with the kind of relationship I have with Great-Grandma Abby."

"I don't know if Mom and I will be able to work things out," muttered Georgia.

"I'm not sure either, but I'm going to go to Maine with you, I'm going to ask my mother to join us at the cottage, and then your mother and you and my mother and I are going to have a talk. A great big one."

"Period, the end?" asked Georgia.

"Period, the end."

# Chapter 20

*Friday, May 6th, 2011*

Georgia sat on the front porch of the cottage and let her gaze drift not across the street to the roiling ocean, gray under a leaden sky, but around the screened-in room at the three women who were sitting with her. She tucked her bare feet under her blue jean–clad legs, crossed her arms, and looked nervously from her mother to Nana Dana to Great-Grandma Abby. She couldn't remember a time, not a single time, when all four generations of women in her family had gathered in one spot.

At first no one spoke, and Georgia sneaked a glance at her watch. Six o'clock in the evening. At that very moment, Natalie and the Hot Chix were rehearsing for their performance at the club in Bar Harbor. Minus one guitar player. Georgia had phoned Natalie from Manhattan on Wednesday to say that she wouldn't be able to play with them. She was pretty certain she wouldn't be asked a second time.

Georgia shifted her gaze to her mother, who was looking at *her* mother, who was looking at *her* mother. "So what are we supposed to do now?" she asked.

"Now," said Dana, turning to her, "we talk. There's far too much in this family that's left unsaid. And there are far too many secrets. It's time for a good airing out."

"When you were a teenager, I practically begged for an airing out," said Abby. "More than once. But you just kept getting more and more distant."

"That's why we need an airing out now. I'm not a teenager anymore, Mother. I see the need for honesty and openness. You were right. You can go ahead and say 'I told you so' if you must, but I'm agreeing with you. We needed to talk then, we need to talk now, and if Francie and Georgia don't talk now as well, then they're going to go down the same road we traveled. Please, let's all of us try to set aside the hurts and concentrate on healing."

Georgia was surprised to see tears in her great-grandmother's eyes.

"Where do we start?" Abby whispered.

"With us, I suppose," replied Dana. "You and me. I was never entirely straightforward with you about why I wanted so badly to leave Maine and return to New York."

"You mean, leave your family," said Abby.

Dana sighed. "I know that's how it felt. To you. But that's not how it felt to me. And it isn't why I had to go back. I had to go back because of Dad."

Abby looked sharply at her daughter. "You said you missed New York."

"You're right. That is what I said. And it was true, but it wasn't the whole truth, which is probably why you never quite believed me. I did miss New York. There were opportunities in New York that I couldn't have while we were traipsing around Maine."

"I did the best I could for you!" exclaimed Abby.

Francie held up her hand. "Let Dana finish, please," she said to Abby. "Do we need to use a Talking Stick?"

Georgia giggled, and even Abby smiled. "Sorry," Abby said. "Go ahead, honey."

"Such as art school," Dana continued. "And I really did miss all the museums, Broadway, everything that Manhattan has to offer. But the truth was that I felt I couldn't be close to Dad unless I was in New York. That was the only place I could feel him, truly *feel* him."

"Honey, we all missed your father," Abby said gently.

"I know, but none of you were standing beside him on the ~~rry~~ when his hat blew off and he jumped into the water to get it. I was the only one who saw that. I was the only one who watched him disappear. I felt as though I should have been able to pull him back. But I —"

"You *couldn't* have!" cried Abby. "You were only a little girl."

"Still. That's how I felt. I watched him disappear, and I wanted him back. When we left New York, I felt like the very last little bit of Dad vanished. It didn't help that I felt like I was suffocating in Maine. But it was Dad I wanted, and I didn't want to tell you that because I didn't want to hurt your feelings. Which obviously I wound up doing anyway."

Abby shook her head, pursed her lips, and silently reached for Dana's hand. "Oh, honey," was all she said.

"Now you see, you two?" Dana went on, turning to Georgia and Francie. "This is exactly why you need to talk now, and be perfectly honest with each other. Things can fester for decades. They can fester forever. So *talk*. Georgia, why don't you start?"

But Francie held up her hand. "If you don't mind, I think I'm the one who needs to start.

Georgia, who had studiously not been looking at her mother, suddenly turned to her. She saw that her mother's hands were shaking. They were shaking so badly that some tea splashed out of the cup she was holding and ran down the side of the couch.

"I can't believe this," Francie said.

"Can't believe what?" Dana asked her daughter gently.

"Can't believe what I'm about to say, and that I never told you about it, never told anyone." She drew in a long breath and let it out shakily. "It's something that happened at the beginning of fourth grade, when I was nine years old."

"What?" Dana looked more nervous than puzzled.

"Remember Erin Mulligan?" Francie said.

Dana's frown intensified. "Erin Mulligan?"

"You don't remember her?"

"No. Why? Who was she?"

Francie looked stricken. "*Dana!* She was the little girl who was kidnapped! The one they never found? The one they assumed had been murdered?"

"Good lord," said Dana. "I haven't thought of her in years."

"Well, I think of her every day."

"Why? You didn't know her."

"No, but . . ." Francie's voice faltered.

"Honey?" asked her mother.

"But about two weeks before she disappeared, a man in a black station wagon tried to kidnap me."

"*What?*"

"It's true." Francie was crying now. "I was walking home from school by myself and a car pulled up next to me and a man inside told me that you had called him and asked him to pick me up and drive me home. I almost got in the car with him. I almost believed him, even though you and Matthew had told me *so* many times never, never to get in a car with a stranger."

"But why didn't you tell us what had happened?"

"Because of what I just said. I felt stupid. And also because the man knew my name. Someone had just called out, 'Francie Goldberg!' and he'd heard. I got away from him then, but he made a threat, and I thought that if he knew my name, then he could come find me. I didn't know what he'd do to me, or to you and Matthew. So I didn't say anything. And then two weeks later, Erin was kidnapped, and after that I *really* couldn't say anything, because everyone would wonder why I hadn't spoken up sooner. If I had, maybe Erin would be safe. So I knew I could never say anything about it."

"Oh my lord," said Dana, wrapping Francie in a fierce hug. "My Francie. My poor Francie."

"Mom," said Georgia with a flash of understanding, "is *that* why you're so afraid? Because you don't want something like that to happen to Richard or Henry or me?"

"I suppose so." Francie sniffed, and reached for her tea-cup. "Ever since then I've felt that it's up to me to keep bad things from happening. I know I can't prevent every-thing, but . . ." She shrugged. "I just wanted to keep you from harm."

"I didn't know," said Georgia in a small voice. "I'm sorry."

"How could you know?" Francie replied and offered her daughter a smile. "It certainly isn't your fault."

"I guess our mothers aren't what they seem to be," said Abby.

"You mean our daughters," said Dana.

"Well, both. But in this case I mean our mothers."

"I don't understand," said Francie.

"I think I do," said Georgia, "but you tell, Great-Grandma."

Abby smiled. "Georgia and I have been keeping a secret of our own. Except ours is a little lighter."

"Yours is," said Georgia in a small voice. "I have another one, as long as we're airing things out, and it isn't light. But you go first."

Abby eyed Georgia curiously, but said simply, "It starts with a stack of old diaries. Why don't you go get them, honey?"

"Really?" said Georgia.

"Really."

So Georgia disappeared into her room and returned to the porch with Nell's diaries.

Abby eyed them. "Five?" she asked.

Georgia nodded.

They took turns telling Francie and Dana about the diaries and Nell and her secret romance. They even showed them the hidey-hole. But when they had settled on the porch again, Abby said, "Apparently, Georgia has a secret to share with us, too. When she told me about the diaries she only showed me four. It appears that there's another."

Georgia nodded. "A final one. The last one Nell kept before she . . ." She looked helplessly at her great-grandmother. "Um, my secret about Nell is sort of awful. That's why I didn't want you to know about it. But now I see that keeping secrets isn't always a good thing. It's just that I didn't want you to . . ." She trailed off. "You know what? There's no real reason for you to know this."

"Tell me," said Abby quietly. "Enough secrets."

"All right." As gently as possible, Georgia related the final months of Nell's life, and finished by saying, "So I don't think she just got sick and died. I think she — I think she killed herself."

Everyone was silent for a long time. They watched Abby, who remained dry-eyed. At last she said, "I guess this explains why my father never wanted to talk about her death. He must have felt responsible, whether he should have or not.

I suppose, too, that he thought he was protecting my sisters and me."

"Your mother really loved you," said Georgia. "You can tell that from all the diaries, but especially the last one. But she didn't know what to do about the way she felt. I think she stayed around longer than she might have if she *hadn't* been your mother."

"If she'd lived today," said Dana, "she could have gotten help. But back then people didn't understand about depression."

"Are you sorry I told you?" asked Georgia.

Abby shook her head. "No. I feel as though I know her better now. And maybe I know my father better, too. Thank you, honey."

Georgia clasped her grandmother's right hand with her left hand, and her mother's left hand with her right hand. She saw her mother reach for her great-grandmother's hand, and her great-grandmother reach for her grandmother's hand.

They sat that way for a long time, in the little cottage on Blue Harbor Lane, four generations linked together. Unified.

# Chapter 21

"How do I look?" Georgia asked Ava.

Ava Norwood stood back and studied her best friend. "Perfect. How do I look?"

"Perfect."

"I can't believe this day is here. I mean, we've been waiting to graduate forever, and now the ceremony is" — Georgia checked her watch — "fifteen minutes away, and suddenly I wish we could do our senior year all over again."

"Really?" asked Ava.

"No. But you know what I mean."

Ava smiled. "I wish I could keep my cap and gown."

"Me, too. Oh, well. You know our parents will take a million pictures of us. That will be almost as good."

Georgia looked around the crowded gymnasium at the seniors, who in five minutes would line up for their graduation, after which they would officially be members of the Barnegat Point Central High School class of 2013.

This time the year before, she and her family had been sitting in the bleachers on the playing field, waiting for Richard and his classmates to file outside, waiting to hear Richard's name called: Richard Burley Noble. With high honors.

*With high honors.* It had been hard to believe. Georgia suspected that Richard had had the hardest time of anyone believing what he had achieved. But he'd spent his junior and senior years working hard, and had been accepted at Colby College. He'd turned his back on a lot of his former friends (Georgia's parents were fond of saying, "Were they ever truly your *friends*, Richard?"), had made a few new friends, and had worked with his physical therapist until he could walk without a limp. He had also told Georgia that he thought about the accident and about Mr. Elden every single day.

Georgia felt a hand on her shoulder.

"Wake up," Ava said. "Come on. It's time to get in line."

Georgia made her way through the room of flapping blue gowns and excited, chattering, laughing, about-to-be graduates. As rehearsed, she took her spot behind Wray Nissen. Ava stood directly behind her. Georgia turned to look at her and burst into tears.

"No! Don't start!" exclaimed Ava. "You're going to make me cry, too. Turn around so I can't see you."

Georgia flashed her friend a trembling smile and turned toward Wray's back. She tried to envision her family in the bleachers outside. Her parents and Henry were there, of course, and so was Richard. He'd been home from his freshman year at Colby for several weeks. All four of her grandparents were also there, and so were Great-Grandma and Orrin. Once again, four generations of Georgia's family were present, a claim that not many of her friends could make. Georgia felt supremely grateful.

She thought back to the night two years ago (two *years* ago) when she, her mother, her grandmother, and her great-grandmother had sat on the porch at the cottage and poured out their secrets. When the evening had ended, Georgia felt like a pond that had been drained. She was empty — although not in a bad way — and, she thought, more tired than she had ever been in her life.

Everyone had been tired, and Great-Grandma had even spent the night, sleeping in Georgia's bed while Georgia slept in a sleeping bag on the floor. When Georgia had awakened the next morning, the first thing she'd thought about was her mother and her secret, about keeping such an awful secret for such a long time. She thought about the guilt that must have built up, and her mother's desire to make things right, or at least her desire never to let anything bad happen again.

In the days that followed, after Nana Dana and Great-Grandma had gone home, and after Georgia had returned to school, she'd sensed a shift in her mother. It was hard to pinpoint at first. She noticed that the atmosphere in the cottage seemed lighter. Then Francie began asking Georgia's father for his opinion, when opinions were called for, and she stopped saying no quite so often. One day Henry asked permission to go on a camping trip with the Quigley boys and their parents, and Mr. and Mrs. Noble simply glanced at each other and said, "Yes."

Georgia's mother had added, "Have fun."

Period. The end.

Eventually, Richard had gone off to college. To Georgia's surprise, he'd said he wanted to leave for his freshman year on his own. Not that he didn't want his parents along on that first day; he just wanted to prove to himself that he could be entirely independent without getting into trouble. And he had been.

Henry had begun his freshman year at BPCHS, and Georgia had sailed through her senior year, continuing guitar lessons with her new teacher and discovering that she enjoyed volunteering at a school for children with developmental delays — using her guitar to draw them out, teaching them songs to expand their vocabulary.

She was remembering the music class she'd taught the previous week, all the children shouting (Georgia really couldn't call it singing, as joyful as it was) "Hot Chocolate" from *The Polar Express*, when once again she felt a hand on her shoulder.

"Georgia!" Now Ava's voice was more insistent. She gave her friend a little shove, and Georgia realized that Wray Nissen was several yards ahead and her classmates were filing out of the gym and onto the playing field.

Georgia ran to catch up, and moments later she was blinking in the bright sunshine of a June afternoon in Barnegat Point, Maine.

Graduation day.

The sun beamed down on the bleachers at the edge of the playing field. Sitting in a line four rows from the front were Georgia's family: Her grandpa Matthew and his wife, Maura, Nana Dana, Great-Grandma Abby, Orrin, Georgia's mother, her father, Richard, Henry, and her other grandparents. They took up an entire row.

Francie blinked back tears as she watched Georgia and her classmates take their places on the playing field. She remembered her own graduation from Princeton High School as she accepted her diploma, and thought of a little girl who would never become a grown woman and would never receive a high school diploma of her own.

Dana remembered her graduation from Manhattan High School for the Arts, an event that couldn't have been more different from the one she was attending now. It had been held in the auditorium of her large New York City school on a rainy day, and her family had traveled from Maine to be there with her. Her beloved aunt Adele had been there, too — everyone applauding Dana as she received her diploma and dreamed of a future as a famous artist.

Abby smiled as she watched Georgia and her classmates. She had graduated from this very same school seventy-three years earlier. The ceremony hadn't been anything like this. For one thing, her class had been just a fraction the size of Georgia's. And although she couldn't see them from the bleachers, she knew that some of the students wore nose rings (Abby would never understand the appeal of looking like a bull), lip rings, and other things she and her classmates couldn't have contemplated in 1940. But still. Here was her great-granddaughter graduating from her very own alma mater — and, unlike Abby, going on to college.

On the playing field, Georgia stood nervously behind Wray and waited to hear his name called. When at last Wray stepped forward, Georgia reached behind her and gripped Ava's hand. Ava squeezed back.

Georgia waited.

"Georgia Eleanor Goldberg Noble," called the assistant principal, and Georgia walked the short distance across the field to the podium that had been set up. Standing in front of the podium was the principal. As she handed Georgia her diploma, the assistant principal added, "With highest honors."

A cheer went up from the stands, a cheer too loud to have come just from Georgia's family, as large as it was. Georgia turned toward the bleachers, waved her diploma in the air, then gleefully shifted the tassel on her cap from the right to the left. She had done it.

She was a member of the class of 2013.


The lights in the cottage on Blue Harbor Lane shone across the scrubby front lawn. Georgia sat on the porch with her mother, Nana Dana, and Great-Grandma Abby. Inside the cottage, and spilling out the back door into the tiny yard beyond were the rest of her family. Georgia heard laughter, heard Richard shout, "Aw, man. No way!" She heard the sound of the refrigerator open and close — and open and close and open and close. She smelled hot dogs and s'mores and the salty ocean air.

She looked at the women who surrounded her on the porch, looked from face to face to face.

"Here we are again," said Great-Grandma. "Four generations."

"Under happier circumstances," said Nana Dana.

"Much happier," agreed Georgia's mother.

Georgia said nothing. She was about to cry for the fiftieth or sixtieth time that day.

Wordlessly her mother handed her a tissue. "You should have seen me when I graduated from high school," she said.

"She was like a faucet," added Nana Dana, and Georgia laughed through her tears.

"What is it with graduation? Why am I so emotional?" she asked.

"Because it's a beginning," said Nana Dana.

"It feels like an ending," said Georgia.

"It's both, I suppose," said Great-Grandma. "But think about what's coming up for you, honey."

Georgia nodded and blew her nose. She actually couldn't wait for what was coming up — and not just college. Before that, there was the summer. Georgia's parents had given her permission to live in Portland for six weeks, teaching music at a school for physically challenged children. She would be earning an actual paycheck and she would be playing her guitar, singing, teaching guitar, and, she hoped, opening up the world of music to children who might not have had any experience with music before.

After that, Georgia would return home for two weeks — two weeks, she suspected, of very sad good-byes with her friends — and then she would be off to Boston where she would attend the Berklee College of Music.

*I'm on my way,* she thought. Her very next thought was, *But what am I on my way to?*

"What am I on my way to?" she said aloud.

No one had to ask what she meant.

"Impossible to know," Great-Grandma replied after a moment. "But whatever it is, we'll be with you every step of the way."

And once again the four generations of women clasped hands.

# Epilogue

*Saturday, May 14th, 2022*

# Abigail Nichols Umhay

When you're an old woman, people bring you things: iced tea, a sweater, a seat in the shade. They're solicitous of you.

They call your name often.

"Great-Grandma!"

"Here, Mother."

"Great-Great-Granny, look at me!"

So I sit in the shade on the bench behind the beach cottage, wearing my sweater, drinking my iced tea, and watching my family. I haven't been to the cottage in several years. Getting here is a bit of a chore. I have to wait for someone to drive me.

"Great-Great-Granny, it's almost time for your birthday cake!"

This is called out by a giddy three-year-old. He belongs to

Richard. This is the first time he's visited the cottage and he's overexcited. The cottage does that to children.

Another voice. "Hi, Great-Grandma."

Georgia lowers herself onto the bench beside me and I edge over slightly to make room for her. I'm still surprised that the airlines let people fly when they're as pregnant as Georgia is.

"Hi, sweetie." I take her hand. "How are you feeling?"

"Fine. I want this baby to be born, though. Alexander and I can't wait for her to get here!"

"She'll be here soon enough."

Georgia lives in California now, a place I've never visited. So far away. Everyone is scattered. Richard and his family live in Michigan, Henry lives in Philadelphia, Francie and George are back in Princeton.

The cottage is a summer cottage again, a vacation destination. A place for holidays and celebrations. Today's celebration is my 100th birthday, an unbelievable milestone, even for the person who has lived every day of those hundred years.

I sit quietly with Georgia and look around at the people in the yard, some of them standing exactly where the rosebushes used to grow. The people I see at first, though, are the ones who are gone now: Orrin, Rose, Adele, Fred, the baby born to Richard and his wife last year.

"Are you okay, Great-Grandma?" asks Georgia.

I realize that my eyes are brimming. I'm a foolish old woman.

I laugh. "I'm fine! Just wool-gathering."

"You're supposed to be celebrating."

The party swirls around me — so many, many people. I'm lucky. I shouldn't be thinking about the ones who aren't here.

Dana approaches, carrying a lawn chair. She's followed by Francie with a matching chair. They place the chairs one at either end of the bench and sit with Georgia and me.

"Here we are again," says Georgia. She turns to her grandmother. "Remember when you hauled me back here after I ran away?"

"How could I forget?"

There's a lull in the party, a break in the talking and laughing and eating. Everyone turns toward the back door. Richard and Henry are edging through it carrying a platter with an enormous sheet cake on it.

The birthday song begins and the cake is set on the table before me.

I hear a child ask, "How come there's only one candle?"

Another child calls, "Make a wish!"

I reach for Dana's hand and Georgia's. Georgia reaches for her mother's hand. We're linked again.

I lean forward and blow out the candle.

"What did you wish?" Georgia whispers to me.

"It's a secret," I tell her, because some secrets really are meant to be kept secret.

# About the Author

Ann M. Martin is the acclaimed and bestselling author of a number of novels and series, including *Belle Teal*, *A Corner of the Universe* (a Newbery Honor book), *A Dog's Life*, *Here Today*, *P.S. Longer Letter Later* (written with Paula Danziger), the Doll People series (written with Laura Godwin), the Main Street series, and the generation-defining series The Babysitters Club. She lives in New York.